Jo's Search

Jo's Search

Dorothy Dart

An Albatross Book

© Dorothy Dart 1984

Published in Australia by
Albatross Books
PO Box 320, Sutherland
NSW 2232, Australia
and in the United Kingdom by
Lion Publishing
Icknield Way, Tring
Herts HP23 4LE, England

First edition 1984

National Library of Australia
Cataloguing-in-Publication data

Dart, Dorothy.
Jo's search.

Simultaneously published: Tring, Herts:
Lion Publishing
ISBN 0 86760 014 4 (Albatross)
ISBN 0 85648 893 3 (Lion)

I. Title.
A823.'3

Typeset by Rochester Photosetting Service, Sydney
Printed and bound in Great Britain by Cox & Wyman Ltd, Reading

Contents

1
Tinoonan

'JO! JO! OPEN THE DOOR, PLEASE. I want you to look after Claire for me for the afternoon while I take Patti to the doctor.'

Joanna Lacey scowled and hurriedly stuck the photograph of Sonia Graham that she had cut out of a women's magazine into her scrapbook and stuffed the book back into the bottom of her wardrobe.

'Jo! Do you hear me?' The door handle rattled impatiently.

'Joanna, unlock the door at *once*. I tell you I must take Patti into town to the doctor. She's feverish and I'm worried about her.' Jo's stepmother, Fiona, spoke again. She sounded pretty angry this time.

It'll be the day when you're worried about me, Jo thought belligerently, then she stopped short. She didn't want any of *her* sympathy or pity. What did she have to come here for anyway, spoiling everything? And now there was not only little Patti, but baby Claire to put up with as well. Everything had been so good when there had been just Jo and her father and they had the whole of Tinoonan Station to themselves — apart from the sheep, horses, dogs and a couple of station-hands, of course.

There was an exasperated sound on the other side of the door, a sound that ended almost in a little sob of despair. Jo shuffled over and unlocked the door.

'Oh, there you are! Please take care of Claire for

7

a couple of hours', Fiona began pleadingly, as she thrust the eight-months-old baby into Jo's reluctant arms. 'Your father's in the dam paddock ploughing and he's got to get it finished so the planting can begin. And I really must take Patti...'

'To the doctor. Yes, I know,' Jo finished sullenly for her, as baby Claire squirmed around and pulled at her hair.

'There's no need for you to stop what you're doing. In fact I'd rather that you keep her in the house — it's a bit windy out. Thanks, you're *such* a help.' Fiona Lacey smiled coaxingly at Jo, who turned to scowl at the baby.

'Stop that, do you hear?' she said, pulling the chubby fingers away from her long blonde hair. This was usually kept in a ponytail, accentuating her thinnish features and pointed elfin nose, but now hung loose to her shoulders, making her look almost pretty. Kids at school called her 'Lanky' because her long arms and legs seemed to have outstripped the growth of the rest of her body. Although she looked awkward and lacked the grace of some girls of her age, she was by no means clumsy. And if her hair was one of her redeeming features, her huge, almond-shaped eyes were another. Deeply blue and very expressive, they gazed out at the world from a permanently sun-tanned face. At the moment they were stormy.

Of course, there was no point in telling Fiona that she had been on the point of going out too, Jo grumbled to herself. She'd planned to climb to the Pinnacle this afternoon to see if there were many kangaroos about on the plains. Dad had promised to take her shooting when she was thirteen — and that was just three weeks away. There were always a few 'roos on Tinoonan, just as there were a few emus, but just lately more seemed to be appearing, driven into the open in search of food because of the

8

prolonged drought. Even so, Jo's dad did not like shooting them unless they were in plague proportions.

For that matter, Jo didn't really like killing things either. But when the kangaroos built up in numbers and ate the wheat and stock-feed, there was really no option. According to her father, shooting was considered to be man's work, but Jo was eager to prove to her dad that she could do anything that a boy her age could do. Besides, when they went shooting, she would have her father to herself again in an activity in which neither her stepmother nor her two little stepsisters could share. And this was what, to her, was important.

Jo placed Claire on the carpet with her own ancient battered teddy bear, and watched the baby as she lifted a ragged paw to her mouth and began to chew it. Down the hall she could hear the sound of her stepmother getting the uncooperative Patti ready.

'Come on, put your shoes on. Hurry now, or we'll miss the doctor. That's the girl,' Fiona encouraged the fretful child.

At last Jo heard Fiona's high heels tap-tapping down the hall. 'We're off now, Jo. There's a bottle of orange juice on the kitchen table for Claire. See you around six,' Fiona called. The screen door slammed shut after her.

For a while Jo just sat there, watching Claire. It was boring being cooped up in the house. She didn't usually spend any more time indoors than was absolutely necessary as she was more at home on Firefly, her filly, or riding with one of the men on the tractor.

She went to the window and looked out at the craggy hill they called the Pinnacle — her favourite spot because of the commanding view it presented of the whole countryside. The wind had died down.

Surely no harm could come from taking Claire for a walk in her stroller and, anyway, they'd be back long before Fiona or Dad came home. Nobody need ever know they'd left the house.

She ran down the hall to the girls' room and found Claire's warmest coat. 'We're going for a walk' she said to Claire, who gurgled happily. Jo popped into the kitchen and picked up Claire's orange juice. She slipped this into the pocket of the jacket she was wearing over her jeans and then she let herself and Claire out through the screen door. Claire grinned with delight as Jo strapped her into the stroller and commenced to push her over the rough, dusty ground.

It was really tough going with the baby stroller; the further Jo went the worse it got. But Claire didn't seem to mind being bumped about like a sack of potatoes. Sometimes Jo had to pick up the stroller and carry it over rocks or little gullies as there was no man-made track to the Pinnacle.

The ascent of the hill itself was gradual but even so it was awkward with the stroller and, after a while, Jo was forced to pause for breath. As she did so, she looked down on the station buildings nestling comfortably between the bottle tree that stood like a plump sentinel on guard and the protective, drooping, willow-like arms of the weeping myall tree.

The house itself was a rambling, wooden, low-set structure, with a wide gauzed verandah on three sides. It had been built by Jo's grandfather when the original Lacey homestead had been destroyed by fire in the 1920s. But now it, too, was showing signs of wear. Some of the stumps had been hollowed by an industrious colony of white ants and the outside walls were crying out for the coat of paint that Jo's dad kept promising to give them when his next wheat cheque came in.

To the front of the house Jo's miserable attempt at a rose garden struggled to exist midst a jungle of weeds. Nearby, as if to taunt the roses, hundreds of neglected purple bougainvillea blossoms cascaded from their rickety trellis over the gate that led into a modest citrus orchard.

The vegetable patch at the side of the house, though, was a different story. It would have to be, Jo thought, with more than a trace of jealousy. Under her hands it had suffered the same fate as the roses but, with the coming of Fiona and the sinking of a new bore which ensured unlimited water supply to the garden, that was *another* thing which had changed. Now nurtured by Fiona as her pride and joy, it was burgeoning with fat, ready-to-be picked peas and beans, carrots and broccoli, cabbages and pumpkins. She was determined, like Jo's grandmother and great-grandmother before her, to be as self-sufficient as possible where vegetables for the dining-table were concerned.

About twelve metres to the left of the house stood the galvanised iron shed housing the vehicles and heavy machinery, while beyond that again stood the split-rail holding yards and the shearing shed. A little to the right of this, level with the house, lay the fowl-run and the men's quarters, the latter being simply a low-set unpainted fibro cottage. This was usually empty but at present was occupied by the sole employee on Tinoonan.

On the other side of the house, where one of the house cows was now wandering listlessly towards the milking bales, stood the old windmill. Overhead a flock of screeching galahs rose in a grey cloud from the branches of the myall tree that shaded the open-sided, hay-filled barn. Further to the right again were the dilapidated stables and horses' yard.

The roofs of all the buildings were painted red, the shed having the word 'Tinoonan' outlined on it

11

in faded white lettering which could be seen, if one looked carefully enough, from the air.

Jo sighed. It all looked so peaceful somehow, so right. She wished she could feel its tranquillity deep down inside her like she used to, only somehow she couldn't. Not any more.

Doggedly she turned back to the climb. Perhaps at the top she'd find the plains thick with 'roos. But she had to *get* there first. It was the only thought that kept her going. What would she find at the summit?

2
The Pinnacle

JO'S PROGRESS WAS SO SLOW that she began to despair of ever reaching the summit of the Pinnacle.

'Somehow I've got to do it,' she muttered determinedly to herself, as she sank to rest again some time later on a large flat rock. And then the thought struck her. The stroller should be quite safe there for a while. Jo did a swift calculation. It would take her about seven minutes, unhampered by the baby and the stroller, to reach the summit if she took the short cut. Allowing for three minutes to look around at the top, then five minutes to come back down, she would need only fifteen minutes altogether.

From the pocket of her coat she took the bottle of orange juice and proceeded to settle Claire down with it in the stroller. She had no idea how long it usually took Claire to finish it but, with a bit of luck, Jo thought she could be well and truly back before Claire had even realised she had gone.

Like a young mountain goat she scrambled up the rocky incline, leaping sure-footedly from rock to rock and then hauling herself up the last two metres until she was at the summit. She was inhaling deeply as her eyes scanned the expansive panorama below. To the north lay the sheep-dotted pastures of Tinoonan. These gave way to low-growing acacia and eucalypt forests that stretched as far as the eye could see. But, much as she loved this view, Jo was fascinated by what lay beyond the horizon.

Much, much further north again lay the fantastic sandstone cliffs of the Carnarvon Ranges. They had stood for centuries like battlements, holding the secrets of probably the same Aboriginal people who had once tramped the plains of Tinoonan away back in the Dreamtime. Jo and her father had camped at the Carnarvon Gorge once. She would never forget the feeling of mystery and awe that surrounded the place. Ever since that time she had loved to sit up here on the Pinnacle and dream about the early days.

There were some Aborigines in her class at school, but they were not like those of her dreams — wild and primitive, with their ritualistic initiation ceremonies and fascinating corroborees. There had still been a few of them around when Jo's great-grandfather had taken up his selection in the 1880s. But, with the coming of more and more white settlers, they had soon vanished, pushed further and further back into the harsh, rugged interior where they had eventually died out. All they left were a few quaint names scattered about the countryside — one of which was Tinoonan — and the priceless art on the walls of caves, to tell the people who came after them that they had ever been there at all. It was sad, Jo thought, that they had to die out so that she could live here today and love the land as they had done before her.

But today there was no time for dreaming — and she could see at a glance there were no 'roos either. Hopefully Jo cast her eyes to the east where the empty paddocks of Tinoonan lay waiting to be planted with wheat and a small tornado of dust alongside the dam in the distance marked the spot where her father was ploughing. But again she was disappointed — there was not a 'roo to be seen. To the south she could see right down to the long, straight road that linked Tinoonan with the rest of the world, but still no kangaroos were visible. The wind was beginning to spring up again and Jo shivered in the icy breeze as she turned her gaze westward, down over a lonely prospector's tent on the coarse, sandy creekbed and across towards the rolling plains.

Her watch told her it was ten-to-five. Jo knew it was a bit early. The kangaroos didn't usually appear to feed until dusk but, with the weather being so dry, she had counted on them being about earlier — especially if they were reaching plague proportions as she had been anticipating. At first sight she could see none in this direction either.

Jo was about to turn dejectedly away, when her sharp eyes caught a movement on the edge of some young oats on the creek flats further along.

'There's one! There's another! Oh, there's dozens!' she exclaimed aloud, excitedly jumping up and down.

Satisfied that her efforts had been rewarded, she turned to look down at the flat rock where she had left Claire. There was still no sign of any little head peeping out of the stroller, so Jo breathed a sigh of relief. Rapidly she began the descent, turning to check on Claire every couple of steps. She was almost down the steepest part and back to the rock, when a strong gust of wind came sweeping across the face of the hill. Jo felt it whipping about her face and tearing at her hair. Pieces of grit blinded her for a moment and, when next she opened her eyes to check on Claire, her heart almost stood still.

The baby had managed to pull herself up onto her podgy legs and was rocking dangerously backwards and forwards on the seat of the stroller. All at once it began to move and Claire sat down with a jolt.

'Oh, why didn't I think to put the brake on?' Jo

15

thought as icy prickles of fear ran down her spine.

'Stop, stop!' she screamed helplessly to the wind, as the stroller rolled relentlessly towards the edge of the flat rock and a ten-metre drop onto rocky boulders below.

'Claire! Claire!' Jo screamed, as she slipped and slid down the rocks, unaware of the cuts and bruises she was inflicting on herself.

Just then a boy appeared from behind a ledge, racing across the flat rock towards the stroller as it lurched dangerously on the edge. In the next second he had grasped the stroller firmly by the handle and was walking over to where Jo was scrambling down the last of the rocks, her breath coming in short, gasping sobs.

'That was a pretty dumb thing to do — to leave a baby alone up here like that,' he said, looking at Jo with accusing brown eyes.

Suddenly the baby looked up at the strange boy and began to cry. Stifling her own tears, Jo picked Claire up in her arms.

'It's all right, it's all right. Don't cry now,' she whispered over and over. She rocked the child backwards and forwards, until at last Claire was consoled by Jo's familiar voice.

'You must think I'm crazy,' Jo whispered after a time.

When the boy made no reply, she went on, 'It's just that I wanted to see if there were any 'roos about. From up there you can see for miles. I didn't mean any harm to come to Claire. I just forgot to put the brake on.' She shivered as she thought of what might have happened to Claire if the boy hadn't appeared at the crucial moment.

'Anyway, thanks for what you did. She might've been killed if you hadn't been there.' Jo turned and buried her face in the baby's shoulder to hide her tears of relief. The awful part about it was that, deep in her heart, she had often wished that something would happen to Claire, Patti and Fiona so that she could have her father back. And now that Claire had nearly been killed she felt as guilty as if she had done it on purpose.

'It's okay. Turn off the waterworks. I was there and she's okay, so don't get uptight, eh?' the boy put in awkwardly.

When Jo still didn't look up, he spoke again. 'Look, I won't blab to anyone if you don't, so you don't have to worry about copping it from your parents.'

At that, Jo raised her head and really looked at him for the first time. She'd seen him about once or twice lately. He came from that prospector's camp down on the creekbed that formed the boundary between her father's property and a piece of no-man's-land. Jo's father, Joe Lacey, was a member of the Shire Council and was anxious to have the Council declare this area a wilderness reserve to keep out the growing tide of itinerant prospectors. Prospectors in his eyes, apart from ruining the ecology, were a constant bushfire threat. Jo had been forbidden, on more than one occasion, to have anything to do with them. But all Jo saw now was a stocky boy about her own age, with freckles and gingery hair and the whitest set of teeth she had ever seen. She noticed them especially now because he was smiling, a warm infectious smile, and soon she was smiling back.

'Fair dinkum? You'll keep it a secret — just you and I?' she whispered.

'Course.'

'Will you shake on it?' Jo went on, unconvinced.

'Sure,' the boy nodded.

They shook hands solemnly.

'What's your name?' Jo asked.

'Karl. Karl Lofts. I live with me Grandpa down

in the camp on the creek. I often climb the hill in the afternoon to look at the sunset, but I'm earlier today.'

'Yes. I recognised you. And I'm Jo Lacey. My father owns Tinoonan,' Jo said simply.

'I know. I've seen you around a lot. When I saw you coming this arvo I thought I'd get into trouble for being on your land, so I hid down the hill. That's how I happened to be here when. . . '

He paused awkwardly, then went on, 'Man! You can ride. I wish I could ride like *that*.' Karl sat down on a boulder and, when he bent his knee, Jo could see his bare skin peeping through a huge hole in his faded jeans.

'Oh, it's nothing,' Jo shrugged self-consciously. 'Can you ride at all?'

'No. Me Grandpa's too poor to afford a horse,' Karl grimaced.

Before Jo knew what she was doing, she found herself offering 'Well, I'll teach you to ride if you like.' The memory of her father telling her to have nothing to do with the prospectors niggled at the back of her mind, but she pushed it away. Hadn't Karl just saved baby Claire's life? Surely she owed him that much. And anyway, she liked him and was lonely for some companionship of her own age.

'Well, I'll have to be getting back now. See that patch of scrub over there? There's a small clearing in the middle of it.' Jo pointed with her hand, carefully selecting a spot which would be well out of view of the house and well away from where her father and the station hand were currently working. 'I'll see you there tomorrow afternoon if you like — after school. I get home on the school bus about four o'clock, so I could be there by half-past. I usually go for a ride about then anyway. So it's a deal. I'll give you your first lesson on Firefly tomorrow,' she finished with a grin.

18

'Aw, great!' Karl's eyes danced at the prospect.

'See you, then,' called Jo as she continued the descent, holding Claire this time and dragging the empty stroller behind her.

She turned to wave when she reached the bottom, but Karl had gone. 'It's as if he never was there at all,' she told herself, and then she reminded herself with a shiver, 'Oh, but he was. He *was* — thank goodness for that.'

3
Unexpected meeting

'YOU'RE VERY QUIET TONIGHT,' Jo's father said to her at dinner that night. 'And what have you been doing to yourself? You've got a nasty cut under your hand. Oh well, you've got a mum who's a pretty good nurse — she'll look after it for you.'

'Oh, it's nothing. I cut it while I was peeling the vegies.' Hastily Jo pulled her hand under the table, away from the scrutiny of Fiona across the table. She wished her father wouldn't keep referring to Fiona as her mum. She wasn't her mum and that was all there was to it.

'Let me see, Jo,' Fiona said kindly.

'No, it's all right. I put some iodine on it when I did it. It's nothing much,' Jo said flippantly and then adroitly turned the conversation around to Patti.

'What did the doctor say was wrong with Patti?'

'Oh, just 'flu, but a nasty attack,' Fiona answered. 'She's to stay in bed for a couple of days. I did appreciate you looking after Claire for me today, Jo,' she finished and turned to her husband. 'It sure is wonderful to have a daughter who is old enough to be such a help,' she said, adding, 'I had no qualms about Claire when I left her with Jo this afternoon. None at all.'

Jo flushed guiltily. Suddenly she found that she had lost her appetite. She turned to her father,

'Please may I leave the table? I've got a lot of homework to do.'

'Well, if you're sure you've had enough to eat, I suppose so. You girls are always thinking of your figure, and milk puddings do put on weight, so they tell me,' her father said in a jovial voice.

'Thanks, Dad. Excuse me,' Jo looked briefly at Fiona, hurriedly rose and left the room.

She was shaking when she got into the hall. She had taken great pains to cover a scratch on her forehead with her hair, but she hadn't bargained on anyone noticing the underside of her hand. And she'd been so careful the way she held her fork. Of course now was the time to tell them the truth about what had happened. But she couldn't face the look of disappointment in her father's eyes and the look of anger she was sure she'd see in Fiona's. And as for telling her father about seeing the 'roos, she no longer had any interest in the adventure she had so long looked forward to.

At the door to Claire and Patti's bedroom Jo paused. Both little girls were asleep. She closed her eyes and imagined the empty cot and her father and stepmother frantic with grief. The baby stirred in her sleep. Quietly Jo tiptoed away to her room and locked the door.

Half-an-hour later, when she slipped out to the bathroom, she overheard her father and stepmother talking as they did the dishes together in the kitchen.

'I'm glad to see you're giving Jo a bit more responsibility with the babies. She's really a reliable kid despite the lack of co-operation she has shown you this past eighteen months,' Jo's father was saying.

'Oh yes, I'm sure she is. I only wish she'd accept me. She still doesn't, you know. You saw the way she acted at the table when I praised her about today. If only she'd accept me as her mother now,

21

but if not that, as a friend. I've tried being nice and I've tried being firm, but nothing I do seems to make any difference,' Fiona replied.

'Just be patient a little longer, my dear. She'll come round in time,' Jo's father rejoined confidently. But Jo knew that she never would. Slowly she tiptoed back to her room and crawled into bed.

The next afternoon Jo was on her way to feed the fowls, when she was surprised to see Mick Fountain step out from behind the myall tree.

'Hi, there,' he said with a smirk at the corner of his mouth.

Fountain was the new station hand her father had hired to replace old Fred McIntosh who was in hospital with appendicitis. He was in his twenties and prided himself on being an ex-bikie from the city. He wore his long, lank hair in a pigtail and had a punk earring in his left ear. Except on really hot days like today, he never discarded his leather bikie jacket that had a dragon with enormous green glass beads for eyes emblazoned on the back.

Jo had never liked the surly way he spoke to her father, nor the impudent look he gave her whenever she passed, nor the way he had of appearing where one least expected him. And as far as work was concerned, he seemed to do it when and where he pleased. She was sure he wouldn't have lasted more than a day working for her father except that, with Fred away, he was desperate for help.

'What do you want?' Jo snapped nervously.

'Yer old man sent me up to the barn for something. But seeing you there, I jus' wondered, could you spare me a few bucks — say forty? I'm a bit short, see, and I need the dough real quick. I gotta pay a small gambling debt,' Fountain drawled.

'Well, why don't you ask my father then? He'll pay you in advance if you're really hard up?' Jo asked, impatient to be rid of the man and off on Firefly to meet Karl.

'But I've already done that and he won't, you see, and I thought you'd rather lend it to me than have me go to yer old man telling *tales*.' The shifty green eyes stared intently at Jo's suddenly ashen face.

'*What* tales?' Jo asked through tight lips.

'Oh just 'bout you up on the Pinnacle yesterday with the baby. It could've turned out real nasty now, couldn't it — 'cept for the boy.' Fountain drawled sweetly.

Jo opened her mouth to reply, but quickly shut it again.

'How... how did *you* know?' she managed to say at last.

'Oh, I seen it all, didn't I? But I happen to think yer a cute chick, so I won't tell yer old man, not if you come good with the dough.' Fountain casually flicked a burr off his pants with one finger.

'But... but I don't have forty dollars in cash,' Jo gasped, setting the tins of laying mash down so that she could wipe her sweaty hands on her jeans.

'Well get it then. Yer old man's got plenty.' The man leaned so close that Jo could smell the stale odour of his sweating body. It made her feel ill.

'But he doesn't give me money like that,' Jo said weakly.

'Well, perhaps you could 'borrow' it from him and tell him later,' Fountain persisted impudently.

'But... but that would be stealing!' Jo burst out.

'Jo! Jo!' Jo had never been so pleased to hear her stepmother's voice. 'Bring me the eggs will you? I'm waiting.'

'Answer her,' Fountain hissed at Jo, slipping back behind the cover of the myall tree.

'I'm just going to feed the chooks now. I'll bring them in a minute,' Jo called back.

'Okay, I'm off now. But I'll be back here

tomorrow night, just on seven. Bring the forty bucks then and I'll keep me mouth shut about what I know. It's up to you,' Fountain shrugged.

Jo's heart was beating like a hammer as she watched him slouch away to the barn. Somehow she managed to feed the fowls and collect the eggs, which she practically threw onto the kitchen table before bolting back outside again.

Firefly was waiting impatiently in the stable which she shared with Mr Lacey's thoroughbred stallion, King.

Ignoring King, Jo went straight to her filly. Soon she had saddled Firefly and was on her back, riding furiously over the paddocks in the direction of the patch of scrub and Karl.

4
Blackmail

'I THOUGHT YOU WEREN'T COMIN',' Karl called out, as Jo reined in and dismounted.

'Not coming? I said I'd be here, didn't I?' Jo retorted hotly.

Suddenly Karl grinned that infectious grin and Jo grinned back. 'Sorry to snap your head off. I guess I'm still a bit uptight today. Well, first lesson coming up. Come over and pat Firefly and get to know her. That's right,' she went on, as Karl put out a tentative hand to caress Firefly's nose.

'Now, step number one. You mount like this,' Jo gave a demonstration and then it was Karl's turn.

'Wow! This is unreal!' Karl gasped when he was astride the horse, his eyes shining.

'Now, hold the reins loosely, not too tight. Pull on the right one just a little if you want her to go right, the left one if you want her to go left and pull back on both if you want her to stop. But I'll lead you first till you get the feel of her.'

All of Jo's troubles were temporarily forgotten in the joy of sharing with Karl one of her most precious possessions. Around and around the clearing Jo led her horse, until Karl felt confident to ride alone. Then with a satisfied smile Jo stood back and watched Firefly briskly cantering around the clearing and through the trees. Before either of them realised it, the shadows had lengthened and it was time to go home.

25

Suddenly, Jo remembered Mick Fountain and her mood changed. Somehow she had to get forty dollars between now and seven o'clock tomorrow night.

'Will you be here tomorrow?' Karl asked hopefully, as he dismounted and patted Firefly's nose.

'Sure,' Jo nodded. She hesitated a moment and then burst out, 'Karl, you wouldn't have forty dollars you could lend me, would you?'

'Heck no, I wouldn't have *four*,' Karl shrugged. 'But what on earth would Joe Lacey's daughter want to go borrowing forty bucks for?'

'Forget it. I shouldn't've asked,' Jo hurried in quickly, adding 'Yep, I'll be here tomorrow. I'll have you riding like a real pro in no time.' She gave a forced laugh, mounted Firefly and, with a hasty wave, began to canter homewards.

All the way home Jo wrestled with the problem of whether or not she should, even at this late stage, tell her father about yesterday's episode on the Pinnacle now that Mick Fountain was involved. Even as she put Firefly in her stall and rubbed her down, she was still unsure. One minute she was rehearsing what she was going to say to her father; the next she couldn't bring herself to do it at all.

'I'm going to tell him right now,' she said aloud, as she heard her father drive up in the Landrover and precede her into the house. But as she walked up the back steps her father was holding forth in the kitchen in heated tones.

'I told that parasite prospector in no uncertain terms that, if he didn't get off that land in a hurry, I'd take out a court order against him until the Council can be persuaded to prohibit prospecting there. There's always somebody camped down there on the creek and, with the weather so dry, I'm darned if I'm going to risk the danger of a bushfire right now simply because of some idiot's carelessness with his campfire. It's all right for them; they can just move on, but we could be wiped out by one of their lousy fires.'

Suddenly all Jo's resolve to tell her father about yesterday crumbled away. He sounded angry, very angry, but not nearly as angry as he would be when he knew she'd made a fool of him, allowing him to go and tell the prospector off just when he ought to be going down there and thanking the old man's grandson for being around and saving Claire's life.

Quietly Jo tiptoed through to the bedroom and took down her piggy bank from its place on the shelf. She prised it open with the point of a pair of scissors and counted the money. She had only fifteen dollars — money she had been saving towards a cassette player. Slowly she picked up the crumpled notes. Fountain had said he wanted all the money tomorrow, and she knew that he meant what he said. Her eyes roamed about the room as she wondered what she might be able to sell. There was her china crinoline-doll bedlamp that had once belonged to her mother, but she could never part with that. There was her old teddy bear, but it was worthless. Then her eyes lit upon her guitar, propped up in the corner. Kathie Wilkinson had always wanted a guitar, but her parents couldn't afford to buy her one. Perhaps she'd buy it for twenty-five dollars.

She went to the hall and listened. Her father was still talking to Fiona who was dishing up the dinner. Patti was wailing because, now that she was feeling a little better, she wanted her stepfather to be a 'horsie' as he often did when he had his evening play with her.

She picked up the telephone and asked the girl on the exchange for the Wilkinsons' number. To Jo's intense relief, Kathie herself answered the phone and Jo spoke in a low voice.

27

'Say Kath, it's Jo here. You know how you've always admired my guitar?'

'Hmmm,' Kathie's noncommital voice mumbled at the other end of the line.

'Well, how'd you like to buy mine for twenty-five dollars? It's in perfect order and cost about eighty dollars new. It's a real bargain,' Jo went on, listening with one ear for her father's approaching footsteps.

There was a long silence. 'Oh, hurry up please,' Jo breathed.

'Okay, it's a deal,' Kathie said at last. 'Bring it to school tomorrow and I'll give you the money.'

'Done!' Jo almost cried with relief. 'Bye now, Kath. The dinner's on the table and I'll have to fly.' She replaced the telephone receiver just as Fiona called out, 'Dinner's ready, Jo.'

5
Prospectors

NOBODY ASKED ANY QUESTIONS when Jo took her guitar to school the next morning. She was often in demand to play it in the music lesson as she had quite a good voice and had been taking guitar lessons since she was ten.

Kathie was as good as her word and produced the twenty-five dollars as soon as she saw Jo with the guitar.

'I still don't know why you want to sell it,' she said, giving Jo a curious look. 'But at that price, it's a steal. Mum said I'd be mad to say no and, anyway, your father can afford to buy you as many guitars as you like.'

Jo turned away to hide her red face. How far from the truth that was! Only the family knew what a struggle it had been to keep Tinoonan going during the drought. Some town people thought that, just because you owned a property, you had to be rich.

Not for the first time Jo wondered what she was going to tell her father when he asked what had happened to her guitar. That it had been lost or stolen? With a bit of luck it would be a while before he even knew it was missing, and by then she might have been able to save twenty-five dollars again and be able to persuade Kathie to sell it back to her for the same price.

The day dragged on. Somehow Jo couldn't keep her mind on her lessons. All she could think of was that tonight she had to meet Mick Fountain and give him the money. The only bright spot to look forward to was Karl's riding lesson after school and even that was a forbidden pleasure. Anyway, she told herself, Karl mightn't want anything more to do with her now, after the way her father had spoken to his grandfather.

But Karl was there waiting for her when she arrived at their meeting place after school. Once again the riding lesson and his company put the thought of Mick Fountain temporarily from Jo's mind.

They were sitting on the dry, sun-baked ground taking a breather when Karl said, 'Have you ever seen one of these?' He produced from his pocket a small piece of topaz.

'Blimey! Did you find it around here?' Jo looked at the stone in amazement.

'No, it came from Mt Surprise up north. There's no topaz around here. But it does belong to me — I found it meself. Pa says it's not worth much 'cause it's got a flaw in it. But it'll fetch around forty dollars. You can keep it if you like.' Karl said with a careless shrug.

'Oh Karl, you mean you want to give me this instead of the forty dollars I asked you for? Oh, I couldn't take it, I couldn't. Anyway... I don't need the money now. I... I've made other arrangements. I had no right to ask you for it anyway.' She hesitated for a moment, then went on quickly, 'Especially after my father told your grandfather yesterday that he had to clear out. Oh Karl, I feel awful about that. I only wish Dad wouldn't be so down on the prospectors, but he feels they are a threat to our property. It's cost him a terrible lot to keep it going through the drought,' Jo's eyes pleaded with Karl to understand.

'Don't worry. We're used to moving on,' Karl

30

said nonchalantly. Then he hastened to add, 'But me grandfather does have a licence to prospect there and we're not camped on your side of the creek.'

'It doesn't make any difference. My father's on the Council and he's going to get all prospecting there prohibited. Karl, I really am sorry. I don't want you to go away,' Jo finished sadly.

'Oh well, if we have to, we have to,' Karl shrugged, trying to hide his true feelings. Then, changing the subject, he said, 'Keep the stone anyway. I'd like you to have it. If you like, I'll take you fossickin' for yourself one day before we leave.'

'Aw, great! That'd be fun.' All at once the possibility dawned on Jo of using the topaz to buy back her guitar but, just as quickly, she cancelled the thought. No, she'd keep it always — in memory of Karl. But maybe, if he took her prospecting, she might be lucky enough to find another stone that she *could* sell. At this thought she brightened considerably.

'Well, if you're sure you don't need it yourself,' Jo raised her eyebrows, as Karl handed her the stone.

'Course I'm sure,' Karl nodded. Somewhere in the distance a crow cawed in its everlastingly monotonous tones, while nearby some animal crashed through the dry undergrowth, disturbed by their presence. Jo lay back and looked up at the white clouds that swirled across the azure blue sky and sighed. Having Karl for a friend was just about the nicest thing that had ever happened to her. She would miss him when he had gone — if he had to go. Perhaps she could persuade her father to change his mind. She'd certainly try. And then she realised with a little stab of surprise that she knew practically nothing about Karl.

'Karl,' she said suddenly, 'Have you left school?'

'No,' Karl shook his head. 'Me grandpa helps me

do correspondence lessons and I'm in Year Nine. Next year, though, when I'm fifteen I'll have to quit school,' he finished matter-of-factly.

'So you're older than I am, although I'm taller!' exclaimed Jo in surprise, adding, 'I'm nearly thirteen. Do you wish you could stay on at school?'

'I reckon,' Karl nodded.

'Well, if I can persuade my father not to send you away, you could catch the same bus to school as I do,' Jo suggested brightly.

'Yes, but we *won't* be here, will we? And anyway, it depends on me pa. He's getting old now and he needs me to help with the heavy work.' Karl showed his muscles and Jo laughed.

'What about your parents, Karl? Are they dead?' Jo persisted after a moment.

Karl nodded. 'Killed in a car crash. I've lived with me grandpa ever since. That was five years ago.'

'Do you miss them much?' Jo almost whispered, feeling she was treading on sensitive ground.

'Yes,' Karl muttered simply. 'Me dad was a minin' engineer, in Central Queensland. I'd like to have been one too. Me mum...'

'Was she pretty, your mum?' Jo persisted again.

'Yes,' Karl's voice was scarcely more than a whisper.

'Mine is. She's a TV star,' Jo said it with her chin held out proudly.

'*Your* mum?' Karl interrupted. 'Baloney!'

'She is so, too. Oh, not my *step*mother. I mean my *own* mother. Her name's Sonia Graham, *the* Sonia Graham. You must have heard of her. She plays Myra Delaney in Young Executives and she's coming up to Brisbane for a week this Thursday with her co-star, Richard Whittaker, to do a promotion for their new mini series. She's also going to appear live on the Channel 6 telethon on

Thursday and Friday nights. I'm just so mad because I'm dying to see her, but we can't get Channel 6 out here,' Jo finished with a grimace.

'Well, I've never seen your mother 'cause I never get to watch any telly anyway. Me grandpa doesn't have one,' Karl said simply with a shrug.

'No, come to think of it, I don't suppose he does.' Jo put her head to one side thoughtfully. Then she rushed on, 'But you can ask anyone. She really is famous and there are always write-ups in the TV and women's magazines about her. That's where I read about her coming to Brisbane. I keep all the cuttings about her in a giant scrapbook along with all of the birthday cards she sends me. I'll show it to you one day. Dad and my stepmother aren't too keen about me keeping it, but they don't stop me. After all, she is my mother even if she did leave dad when I was only one year old,' Jo finished forlornly.

'Boy!' Karl gasped. 'How could she do a thing like that?'

Jo shrugged. 'She was an out-of-work actress filling in as a night-club singer when Dad met her down in Surfers Paradise at a party. They got married soon after. Then one day someone, her manager I suppose, rang from Sydney and offered her a job in television. She said she was coming back, only she never did. Then she and my father got a divorce and a year and a half ago Dad married Fiona.'

'Don't you like your stepmother, then?' Karl asked softly.

'She spoilt everything when she came here. Dad and I were so happy together.' Jo's eyes looked stormy.

'You might've been happy, but perhaps your father wasn't,' Karl put in with surprising wisdom.

'He was so. What would you know about it?' Jo cut in angrily and then she stopped. 'Sorry for biting your head off again. How about a race to the creek?'

'You're on!' yelled Karl, leaping to his feet and taking off like a hare.

'Okay, okay, you win!' laughed Jo as, red-faced and panting, she caught up with Karl who had not only beaten her to the creekbank, but had leapt onto the coarse river sand and sat grinning up at her.

'Hey there!' Jo turned to see a whiskered, bent-up old man walking towards them carrying a spade.

'Hi, Pa, this is Jo Lacey. She's been giving me another riding lesson.' Karl introduced Jo, who was surprised to see how the blue eyes twinkled in the old, weather-beaten face.

'Charmed to meet you, Miss Lacey,' he said, making a thing of bowing and lifting his old straw hat. 'I had the pleasure of making the acquaintance of your father yesterday,' he went on.

Jo looked at him closely to see if he were angry, but the blue eyes still twinkled mischievously.

'Yes, I know. I . . . I'm sorry that my father was mad with you yesterday. It's just that we can't risk a bushfire or anything.'

'Aw, I know that, lassie, don't worry. An' I'll tell you as I told your father. I'm as careful with a match as a giraffe is not to yell at a football game.' The old man leaned on his spade and looked at her.

'I'm sure you are, Mr . . .?'

'Lofts,' the old man filled in for her.

'I'm sure you are, Mr Lofts, but my father has had bad experiences with prospectors before. Anyway, I'll do my best to try to get him to let you stay on. How long did he give you before you had to be gone?'

'Ten days to be exact, lassie. 'Tis such a pity. I was just getting onto some interesting stuff too,' Grandpa Lofts replied, looking around regretfully.

'Oh, Pa, you're always saying that,' Karl broke in teasingly.

34

'No, no, it's God's truth. I swear it,' the old man nodded his head seriously.

'Well, I promise you I'll see what I can do.' Jo laid a hand on the old man's arm and he smiled gratefully at her.

'I do appreciate that, m'dear,' he said, nodding his head and taking out his handkerchief to wipe his perspiring brow. 'Now have you time for a cuppa before you go? The billy's on the boil.'

'Sure,' Jo grinned and instinctively she knew that, whatever her father said about this old man, he was a man of his word and he would never do anything to endanger their beloved Tinoonan.

'Jo's real mother is a TV actress,' Karl told his grandfather, when the three of them were sitting around Grandpa Lofts' campfire, drinking tea from large enamel mugs.

'Is she then?' Grandpa Lofts' bushy eyebrows rose in surprise. 'And do you plan to follow in her footsteps?'

'Oh no,' Jo put in hastily. 'I'm not pretty enough and anyway I'm never leaving Tinoonan.' She looked around with a wide sweep of her arm.

'So the land is in your blood, eh? Got any brothers or sisters?' Grandpa Lofts asked.

'Only two little stepsisters.' Jo flashed a guilty look at Karl. Had he told?

'My father and mother are divorced and my father married again. My stepmother already had a little girl called Patti and now there's baby Claire as well.' Suddenly Jo found herself telling Grandpa Lofts all about how unhappy she had been since her father remarried. She even told him about the episode on the Pinnacle the day before yesterday and how she had often wished there had not been any Claire or little Patti or Fiona.

'I've never told anyone this before, but sometimes I've wished they were all dead. But the other day, when Claire could have been killed if it weren't for Karl,' and she flashed a grateful look in Karl's direction, 'I knew I *did* care about her after all. I felt as dreadful as if I had actually pushed her over the cliff.' Jo finished and bit her finger nails anxiously as she waited for Grandpa Lofts' reaction.

'Well, lassie, it didn't happen. And just thank God that it didn't,' Grandpa Lofts said gently at last.

'What's God got to do with it? He hasn't shown much interest in me up till now. After all, he let my mother go off and leave me, didn't he? Surely he could have stopped her?' Jo looked up at Grandpa Lofts with intense, hurt eyes.

'Yes, he could I guess, but he gives us all free will and we're allowed to use it. After all, he doesn't force us to believe he exists if we don't want to. It's up to us. And he has given you a new mother now, hasn't he? Only you don't want to accept that. Sometimes, you know, we have to meet God halfway for him to be able to help us. It wasn't easy for us to accept the death of Karl's parents, but eventually we had to adjust and accept what couldn't be changed.'

Jo opened her mouth to speak, but Grandpa Lofts hurried on. 'Oh, I can see that you're a fighter, lass, and I admire someone with spirit. But it's no use fighting all the time.' The old man patted her hand gently with his gnarled brown one and Jo felt tears pricking her eyelids.

'Oh, I wish I had a grandpa like you,' Jo sighed.

'Well for that matter, I've often wished I had a granddaughter just like you, so let's pretend that I am your grandpa and you are my granddaughter.' The warm blue eyes seemed to gather Jo into an ocean of love and, although she couldn't go along with what he said about God, Jo knew he was a very wise old man whom she respected enormously.

Suddenly she looked at her watch. 'Strike! Is that the time? I'll have to scram,' she exclaimed and, rising from her seat on the log, she held out her hand to Grandpa Lofts. 'See ya, Pa. May I come again soon?' she said.

'Of course, lass. Goodbye.' Grandpa Lofts shook her hand and then Jo turned to go.

'I'll come with you as far as Firefly,' said Karl and together they walked away from the old man who watched them silently.

It was good for the lad to have a companion his own age. Good for the girl, too. She was so hurt and angry inside. He sighed and shook his head. Such a pity he and Karl would have to be moving on so soon. Still, he had always found God to be sufficient for his needs and he didn't doubt that he would prove sufficient now.

6
Decision

IT WAS A COLD NIGHT. Jo shivered in her cotton shirt and old blue jeans. It had not been difficult for her to get away, as she always fed the dogs straight after dinner. She took the dogs' tin plates to the tap, washed them, then filled them with their meat. She hosed out their water tin and, as she did so, tried anxiously to make out whether or not she could see a figure in the darkness under the myall tree beside the barn.

Nervously she patted her pocket to make sure that the money was still there. Yes, she could feel the bulge of it — she had counted it out carefully just before dinner.

Furtively she dashed away from the house, down towards the tree but, before she reached it, Mick had materialised out of the shadows and was standing there with his hand held out.

'There you are — forty dollars.' Jo flung the roll of notes into his hand and turned to run.

'Hey, cool it — not so fast,' Mick called after her.

'Look, I have to go. What is it now?' Jo turned impatiently.

'Well, it's like this. I made a little mistake. Actually it's eighty bucks I need.'

Jo gasped. 'Forty is what you told me and I've gone to no end of trouble to get it.'

'Aw well, it'll do for the time being. Just bring the other forty the day after next, eh? That should give you plenty of time,' Fountain drawled.

'I can't. I tell you I can't get another forty dollars so soon,' Jo almost sobbed.

'Oh well, suit yourself. You can if you really want to — it's up to you, like I said before. Forty dollars, day after next at the same time, or I tell yer old man,' Fountain persisted.

'Oh you... you beast,' Jo gasped, and turned and fled back to the safety of the house.

Somehow she went through the ritual of helping with the dishes and mechanically replying when her father or stepmother spoke to her, but deep inside she was wondering all the time what else she could sell.

She went to bed early, but she tossed and turned for hours. When she eventually did fall asleep it was only to dream that she was running down a corridor pursued by Mick Fountain and, at the far end of the corridor, a blank wall cut off any means of escape. She woke up in a lather of sweat, relieved to find it was only a dream.

It was then that she remembered the piece of topaz that Karl had given her and how he'd offered to take her fossicking for herself. Perhaps she could ask him to take her tomorrow? She might just be lucky enough to find a stone of value that she could sell. She slept peacefully after that but rose late, with only sufficient time to gobble down her breakfast and feed Firefly her oats before running off for the school bus.

It was ten-past-four when Jo walked in from school, tired and irritable from the heat. She slung her school bag onto the kitchen floor, said 'Hi' to her father and Fiona who were sitting at the table having their smoko, then went to the refrigerator for a drink of cold milk. She had scarcely lifted the glass to her lips when, from the direction of her bedroom, she heard a crash of breaking china. Banging the mug down onto the table and spilling some of the milk, Jo dashed into her room to find her precious crinoline-doll bedlamp smashed to pieces on the floor and Patti looking up at her, her wide brown eyes saucers of apprehension.

'You little brat!' Jo swooped on the child, shaking her until her teeth chattered. 'What do you mean by coming in here like this when I'm not here. Look what you've done. It's ruined . . . ruined,' Jo yelled and she slapped Patti across the face with her hand.

Patti's screams brought both her parents running.

'Patti! Patti!' cried Fiona, dragging her little daughter away and beginning to comfort her.

'Joanna!' Jo's father thundered. 'You ought to be ashamed of yourself, belting into your little sister like that.' He turned and wagged his finger sternly at Patti who still clung to her mother for protection. 'You were a very naughty girl to come in and touch the lamp, but Jo,' he went on, turning back to his older daughter, 'you are old enough to realise that she didn't mean to break it. You were being far too severe on her. After all, she's only three and the bedlamp can easily be replaced.'

Jo opened her mouth in dismay. 'But Dad, that's not the *point*! That lamp was the only thing I had that belonged to my own mother. It was so precious to me.'

Jo's father exchanged a meaningful glance with Fiona, who turned and left the room with the still sobbing Patti. He waited until they were out of earshot, then he said, 'Don't you think it's time you stopped putting your mother on a pedestal in this way?'

'No, no I don't. Sonia Graham's my mother and nobody else,' Jo burst out, white-lipped.

'Oh Jo, Jo! She never writes. She never comes to see you. What makes you think she cares?' Jo's father said quietly.

'But she *must* care. She never forgets my birthday,' Jo returned.

'Oh, that!' Jo's father opened his mouth as if he were going to say something more. Then he thought better of it and started to reason gently with Jo. 'Look, honey, when I brought Fiona here I at least thought you'd be good friends. She's young, only fifteen years older than you. She's attractive and fun to be with. I did it as much for your sake as for mine. You're growing up. You need a woman's touch, Jo — a woman like Fiona.'

'I do not need her,' Jo said emphatically, at which her father shrugged, turned and abruptly left the room.

Jo sat on her bed and stared at the broken pieces of china littering the floor. She had thought her father would have understood how important the bedlamp was to her. But in this, as in everything else, he was on their side. Everyone was against her.

To comfort herself she went to the wardrobe and took out her scrapbook. As she dwelt on the pictures of the beautiful, smiling Sonia Graham, she started to feel better. Surely this lovely smiling woman, her own mother, would welcome her with open arms if she knew how unhappy she was? It was then that she made her decision to leave Tinoonan for good and, having done so, her mood of depression lifted and she felt strangely elated.

She was surprised at how easily she had come to the decision, having always loved the place so much. But really, when one didn't feel wanted, it made it less complicated somehow. And with Karl and Grandpa Lofts moving on soon life on the station would be unbearable without them. The only thing she really regretted was having to leave Firefly. But even for that there was a solution.

Suddenly she was aware of the mantle clock in the lounge striking the half-hour. She leapt to her feet

41

with a gasp of dismay. It was half-past five! Poor Karl, would he still be waiting? She had to see him before she left. He was the only person who was going to be allowed into her secret.

Hurriedly she changed into her old blue jeans and riding shirt and dashed out of the house to the stable. Today the chooks would have to wait to be fed — she had more important things to do.

Firefly greeted her with her usual whinny of delight as Jo burst in like a whirlwind. As the filly's faithful eyes looked at her, a sob arose in Jo's throat. How could she exist without Firefly? That was going to be the hardest part of all.

'I don't know how I'll bear it without you,' she whispered as she hugged Firefly's neck, her tears falling onto the filly's brown coat. But there wasn't much time to feel sorry for herself. They'd be calling her to do the chores soon and she had to catch up with Karl before he gave her up and went home. Somehow she didn't fancy facing old Grandpa Lofts today. He might even try to stop her carrying out her plan. After all, he was an adult and it was amazing how adults stuck together about certain things.

A few minutes later Jo was galloping out of the stockyard gate and away in the direction of the scrub which had become her regular meeting-place with Karl.

7
Departure

As jo approached the clearing, her eyes sought in vain for Karl's stocky figure. So, he'd given her up as a bad job. Even he had lost faith in her. Oh well, there was nothing for it but to go to his grandpa's camp.

As she rode past the Pinnacle, she looked up. Suddenly her eyes caught sight of a movement high up. She cantered closer and the figure waved. She waved in return.

At the base of the hill, she leapt off Firefly and looped her reins over the branch of a sapling. Soon she was scrambling up, following the route she had taken three days ago. She kept her eyes averted from the ledge over which Claire might have fallen but for Karl, and soon she was within speaking distance of him.

'Hi!' Karl called, as Jo hauled herself up the last steep stretch. 'When you didn't turn up, I thought I'd come here instead to watch the sunset. Look, isn't it unreal!' He gestured away to the west where the sun shone like a red ball in the crimson sky.

To his surprise, he saw tears spring to Jo's eyes.

'It. . . it's just too beautiful for words,' she replied. 'It's just like I always imagined the entrance to the land at the rainbow's end would look.'

'The land at the rainbow's end! There's no such place,' Karl argued matter-of-factly.

'Oh, but there is if you believe in it. At least

according to this fairytale I had when I was little, there is. I used to beg Dad to read it to me every night for ages.' Jo's voice trembled, but she bit her lip firmly and went on.

'You see, it was about two orphans, who were unhappy in this world because nobody loved them. One day after a terrible storm a beautiful rainbow appeared. And swinging on the rainbow there was a rainbow fairy who told them if they could find the land at the rainbow's end, they would find eternal happiness.

'Well, they set off together and, after lots of adventures, they came to this beautiful red and gold land. Actually the pictures in the book looked just like that.' Jo paused and looked toward the west again. 'The real name for this land was Love and, once the children entered this land, they were never unhappy again because there was always heaps of love for everyone.' Jo stopped and was silent.

This time Karl didn't laugh. He was too aware of her trembling hands and her white face.

'It sounds a bit like heaven is supposed to look,' he said soberly.

'Now who's talking about believing in fairy stories?' Jo put in cynically.

'Heaven isn't a fairy story. It's real. I don't know where it is exactly, but it does exist. The Bible says it does — and everyone who believes in Jesus will live there one day with God,' Karl retorted quickly.

'Well, right now I've got more important things to talk about than to argue whether there's a heaven or not.' Jo turned away with an impatient gesture.

For a moment there was an awkward silence. Then Karl burst out, 'Jo, what's bugging you?'

'You've got to swear to secrecy before I tell you,' Jo turned back to him seriously.

Impatiently Karl nodded. 'Don't be a nurd; you already know you can trust me.'

'Yes, you are the best friend I have in the world and that's why I want you to know. Tomorrow I'm going to begin my search for the land at the rainbow's end. I'm leaving Tinoonan, Karl, and I'm never coming back.'

'What! But you said only yesterday that you'd never leave Tinoonan!' Karl exclaimed, his good-natured face clouding with dismay.

'A lot has happened since then,' Jo put in evenly. 'I'm going to Brisbane to find my mother and I'm going to live with her from now on.' And then she told him about the happenings of the afternoon, the smashed bedlamp, what she saw as the rejection of her father and how Mick Fountain was blackmailing her over the incident with Claire.

'The rotten mongrel!' Karl burst out when she had finished. 'You shouldn't have given him anything. Blackmailers are the scum of the earth, my pa says.'

'But I didn't know. I thought he truly wanted the money to pay a gambling debt. I didn't dream he'd keep coming wanting more,' Jo replied quickly. 'Anyway, he won't be getting it,' she finished with a hard little laugh.

'But Jo, you can't just disappear. Your father will be out of his mind with worry,' Karl tried to reason with her. But her mind was made up.

'When... how do you plan to leave then?' Karl asked at last.

'I'll get the school bus into town as usual and then, instead of going to school, I'll catch a passenger coach to Brisbane,' Jo replied easily.

'But... what are you going to use for money?' Karl interposed.

'Aha, that's where you come in. I'm sorry, Karl, but I'm going to have to sell your topaz. I don't want to, but there's nothing else for it. I'll go direct to Mr Stringer — he's the jeweller in Canobie. I

45

know he'll give me good value for it. I only hope it covers the cost of the bus fare.' Jo stopped for breath.

'Jo Lacey! If I'd known you were going to use it for this, I'd never have given it to you,' Karl exploded. 'It's wrong what you're planning to do. You ought to just tell everybody the truth, face the consequences and in time everyone would forget it,' Karl argued.

'No way, Karl, it's too late for that,' Jo muttered sadly. 'Besides, now that my mind is made up, I'm quite excited at the thought of meeting my mother. Actually she lives in a big house in Sydney and she's got pots of money so, once I get to her, I'll be okay.' Jo was adamant.

'Well, if you're set on doing this, how long do I have to keep quiet after you've gone?' Karl asked after a pause.

'Twenty-four hours should be enough. I don't care what you do after that. I'll be with my mother then. Don't you see, Karl? I'll have found my rainbow's end,' Jo paused dramatically, then went on, 'Maybe I will become a TV star, too, and be famous one day after all. Who knows?' She finished with a toss of her head, then gave a little laugh as she looked ruefully at her oversized hands and feet. 'Well, you've heard of the ugly duckling, haven't you?' she added.

Karl, who looked upon Jo as anything but an ugly duckling, was lost for words. Jo mistook his silence for agreement.

'Anyway, beauty's only skin deep so they say,' she shrugged flippantly. Then she became serious again.

'Karl, please tell your Pa I am really sorry I haven't had time to convince Dad to drop his hate-campaign against the prospectors. And Karl, I do have one more thing to ask of you — I do this because I know you love her almost as much as I do. I want you to have Firefly. Maybe your grandpa can continue your lessons.'

'Aw, come off it, Jo,' Karl burst out, dumbfounded. 'Your father wouldn't let me keep her for one thing.'

'Karl, Firefly's mine to do with as I choose. And she likes you. She won't miss me so much if you take her with you. No, don't argue. I promised you I'd have you riding like a pro, didn't I? How are you going to do that without a horse?' she finished with a little laugh.

When Karl still was reluctant to agree she went on, 'Look upon it as payment for what you did for Claire. I'm going to post a letter to my father telling him where I've gone. I'll tell him in the note that I've given Firefly to you, so you needn't worry about that. Well then, I guess that's all I have to say, so it's time to say goodbye.' Jo stood up and held out her hand to Karl in a mannish fashion.

Karl took her hand for a moment in his. 'Goodbye, Jo. I . . . I shall always remember you,' he said softly.

'You too. I'll write if you like, care of the post office in Canobie. Check there before you move on. Goodbye then, Karl.'

Having said this, Jo turned away quickly. The sun had practically disappeared now and the crimson sky had changed to mauve. 'Goodbye Tinoonan,' Jo whispered with one last sweeping look and, without another word, she turned and began to descend the rock. Mutely, Karl followed. Even when they reached the bottom and Jo handed Karl Firefly's reins, there was no further conversation between them.

Torn between the desire to stop Jo doing this crazy thing, and yet having made his promise to keep silent for twenty-four hours, Karl watched with

47

a troubled frown as Jo ran off into the trees like a hunted rabbit.

When Jo returned it was quite dark. Most of the fowls had perched for the night, but she eased her conscience by throwing them their mash anyway and collecting the eggs.

As she passed the stable, the sight of Firefly's empty stall cut her to the heart, but she convinced herself that her filly couldn't be in better hands.

Dinner was a silent meal. Fiona kept trying to act normally, but underneath Jo knew she was fuming. And Patti, for her part, hardly dared look at her. Jo's father alone tried to make conversation, but in the end even he gave up and concentrated morosely on his meal.

After she had helped with the dishes, Jo asked to be excused early for the night and went to her room. She had expected to find it just as she had left it — littered with pink china pieces and fragments of glass — but it had all been cleaned up. A sound behind her caused her to turn to see her father's massive frame filling the doorway.

'Fiona cleaned everything up. I hope you won't forget to thank her. She's very upset at the whole sorry business and has offered to buy you another bedlamp.'

'That's very nice of her,' Jo heard herself say politely, but inwardly she was thinking that she wouldn't need it.

Then suddenly, looking at her father standing there as he had done so often before, Jo felt like a little girl again. All at once she wanted to fling herself into his arms and tell him everything. But then he spoke, spoiling the picture.

'Oh Jo, what's happened to you? You're not the happy girl you used to be.' He paused, then went on, wiping his hand across his furrowed brow, 'Perhaps I ought to send you away to school.'

'If that's what you want,' Jo said levelly, her heart sinking with despair. If she had never known it before, she knew it now: they both wanted to be rid of her. It *had* to be Fiona's idea. Her father would never have tolerated the thought of sending her away to school in the old days.

He stood there a few more minutes, an awkward silence hanging between them.

'Goodnight,' he said at length and, when she still did not answer, he turned on his heel and left her alone.

After he had gone Jo sank weakly onto the bed, the tears rolling down her cheeks. But at length she had cried all the tears she had to cry and, realising that she still had lots to do if she were to leave Tinoonan tomorrow morning, she began to busy herself.

First she took a pad and biro and wrote her father a note telling him where she was going. She also explained that she had given Firefly to Karl as a present for having saved Claire's life. Then she took her school books out of her bag and stowed them safely in the wardrobe, replacing them with an old pair of jeans, a sloppy joe and an old peak cap that had once been her father's. This done, she breathed a sigh of satisfaction and went to take a shower.

8
Brisbane

THE NEXT MORNING JO AWOKE EARLY.
A tingling sensation passed through her thin frame
at the thought of the adventure that lay ahead.

She forced herself to act normally and eat
breakfast. For once she did not have to run to be at
the gate in time for the school bus.

When the bus deposited the children at the school
gate, Jo waited so as to be the last in the queue.
Nobody even gave her a second glance as she dashed
behind the bus and over the street to Mr Stringer's
jewellery store.

The shop was open and only Mr Stringer was on
the premises.

'How much would you give me for this?' Jo asked
at once, holding out the topaz.

'Well now, let's have a look. You're Joe Lacey's
girl, aren't you?' he raised his eyes and peered at her
over his strange half-moon spectacles.

'Yes,' Jo felt her knees shake. Don't tell me I'm
not going to get any further than this, she thought
wildly.

'Found this on your place, eh?' Mr Stringer was
clearly impressed.

'No. A friend gave it to me.' Jo shook her head
and tried to look normal.

'I was going to say that if you've got any more of
these lying about, your dad would do well to join the
prospectors he's so keen on throwing out,' he went

50

on, as he examined the stone under a strong light.

Jo smiled weakly, wishing he'd get on with the business in hand.

'I'll give you fifty dollars for it. Might be able to facet it and make it into a small ring,' Mr Stringer said at last.

'Fifty!' Jo was breathless with excitement. 'Is it a deal then? I'll take the money, thanks.'

Mr Stringer shrugged, went to his till and counted out ten $5 notes.

'Oh thankyou, thankyou Mr Stringer,' Jo burst out ecstatically.

'Off you go then or you'll be late for school,' Mr Stringer laughed good-naturedly as Jo literally raced out of the shop.

At first she walked in the direction of the school, but only as far as the Ladies' Rest Room where she changed out of her school clothes. Then she put on her jeans and red sloppy joe. When she looked into a mirror after having wound her hair into a knot on top of her head and completing her disguise with the peak cap, Jo felt satisfied that she could pass anywhere for a boy of thirteen or fourteen.

Once dressed, she took out the letter she had written telling her father where she was going and hastily added a postscript: he might pick up her bag and school clothes at the Ladies' toilet if he so desired. She couldn't help feeling it was irresponsible to leave her things in a public building like this, but she couldn't risk leaving them anywhere else. Then she walked to the Post Office, bought some stamps from the stamp vending machine and posted the letter.

At the bus depot a new clerk served her. She had purposely waited for him to attend to her for fear she was recognised by Mrs Beazley, who had been in charge of the bus depot bookings for as long as Jo could remember.

As Jo watched the people arriving for the bus, she was pleased to see that none of them were familiar to her. Nevertheless she spent a nerve-wracking fifteen minutes in a corner with her head buried in a magazine, her precious ticket clutched firmly in her hand.

At last the young clerk called for everyone to board the bus. Jo put down her magazine and, with head down, hurried towards the door in an attempt to be the first in the queue. At the door, however, she collided with a plump lady who was carrying a heavy suitcase. A moment later Jo was sitting astride the suitcase on the floor, with the plump lady on top of her.

'Oh my dear, I'm terribly sorry,' the lady was saying, as she was helped to her feet by one of the other passengers.

'No, no, it's all right. It was my fault,' Jo objected, red-faced.

'Not at all. I should have been looking where I was going. It's this heavy suitcase. It's an awkward thing to carry.'

By this time the other eleven passengers had boarded the bus and the driver had finished loading their luggage.

'Now, may I take this for you, madam?' he looked towards the woman as he picked up her suitcase. She nodded gratefully and smiled at Jo as he said, 'You and your lad go ahead and find your seats.'

The lady looked around for Jo's travelling companions and, seeing none, said, 'You're travelling alone then?'

Jo nodded.

'Well we'd better do as the driver said. Come on, my *lad*,' she added, her eyes twinkling at the driver's mistake.

Jo liked the lady at once. Obviously she had a

sense of humour for she had heard her speak and knew that Jo was a girl.

'Would you like to occupy the seat next to me?' she asked as they walked down the aisle. 'I must admit I like to have somebody to talk to.'

'Okay,' Jo nodded, determined for the driver's sake to keep up the pretence that they were together. After all, maybe Mrs Beazley had recognised her in the melee at the bus terminal and would ring her father. He might phone some stopping place along the road and have her sent back.

'We'd better introduce ourselves,' the lady began when they had got themselves settled. 'My name is Martha Patrick, Mrs Martha Patrick. I've been out to visit my brother who lives at a little railway siding called Fenn's Pocket. He's a ganger, you know. I live on a cane farm with my husband near Cairns in North Queensland and tonight I'm catching the plane home. Home!' she sighed, 'I just can't wait to get back to all that green after the red bulldust and dry heat of Fenn's Pocket. I don't know how *anyone* lives there. But still my brother likes it and he doesn't seem to mind the dust and flies.'

As Mrs Patrick chatted on about her home and her brother's lot at Fenn's Pocket, Jo listened with interest. The further they drove away from Canobie, the more relaxed she felt. Getting away had been a piece of cake. She was sure this was a good omen. Everything was going to be all right.

As every turn of the wheels took her closer to the realisation of her dream of finding her own land of happiness at the end of the rainbow, Jo became more confident and excited. Any qualms she might have had that Karl had been right and she ought to tell her father the whole story were quieted. Of course she was doing the right thing, the only thing — and what's more she was beginning to enjoy it.

Fired by this new confidence, her tongue loosened

53

up and soon she was telling Mrs Patrick that her parents were divorced and she was on her way to visit her mother who was a TV star, presently visiting Brisbane. Of course she didn't mention that she had run away from home and was playing truant from school, but she nearly burst with pride when Mrs Patrick said she had actually seen Sonia Graham on the television.

By the time they pulled in at a motel — with so many pot plants in the vestibule that it looked like a jungle, as Jo laughingly whispered to Mrs Patrick — Jo and Mrs Patrick were great friends.

It was during lunch, which they shared at a small table for two, that Jo saw a policeman come into the dining room and glance casually around at the patrons. Hastily she turned her head to the side and her throat went dry. Then, murmuring some excuse about feeling suddenly sick, she rose from the table and walked, although her legs felt like jelly, to the rear exit door.

She expected to hear him call out to her, but he didn't. Nevertheless she spent the remainder of the lunch stop out in the backyard. It was only when Mrs Patrick came to tell her that the bus passengers were making preparations to leave, that she dared to return.

As she walked with the others out of the vestibule, she saw the policeman driving away in his marked police car and she breathed easily again.

'Do you feel all right now?' Mrs Patrick asked her kindly, as they boarded the bus again. 'Such a pity you couldn't finish your lunch.'

'I'll be okay now. Just a little travel sickness, I think,' Jo said, blushing at the lie as she gratefully sank into her seat and the bus driver started up the motor.

As they entered the outskirts of Brisbane, Jo felt she could hardly contain her excitement. She had been here only once before when she had been five, so she didn't remember too much about it except that everyone seemed to be in such a hurry. That, at least, hadn't changed.

In the gathering darkness Jo kept her nose pressed against the glass window of the bus, overawed by the flashing lights, the tall buildings and the dense traffic. As they had drawn closer to the coast, the dry heat of the west had been dissipated and replaced by cooling sea breezes. Now that they had reached the city, a light misty rain was beginning to fall.

At last the bus drew into the terminal and Jo scrambled to her feet, following Mrs Patrick down the aisle.

'Now don't forget, my dear, if you're ever in the north you come and see us. We're in the Cairns telephone book, so give us a ring. It's been really delightful having your company. Every time I see Sonia Graham on the telly from now on I'll think of you. I never knew a real TV star's daughter before. Well, goodbye dear,' she said, giving Jo a quick kiss on the cheek.

When nobody came forward to claim Jo, Mrs Patrick turned back to her. 'You are sure your mother will be here soon?' she inquired with a note of concern.

'Sure, I'm sure. If she can't make it herself, she'll send somebody else.' Jo lied firmly. 'Goodbye Mrs Patrick. And thanks for everything.' She smiled bravely and, with a growing sense of loneliness, watched Mrs Patrick walk away towards a row of gleaming taxis. There she turned again and beckoned to Jo.

'Perhaps something has detained your mother. It's rather out of my way, but if you like I can drop you off at the TV studios on my way to the air terminal. I have time and I don't like leaving you here alone.'

'Oh Mrs Patrick, that'd be terrific!' Jo burst out gratefully.

Now that it was time to say goodbye to her friend, she was loathe to let her go. And she didn't really have a clue which way to go to find the Channel 6 television studios where she hoped to find her mother.

'Okay, then, hop in.' Mrs Patrick gave the address to the driver after he had stowed her suitcase in the boot and away they went, whizzing through the traffic along the wet, shiny streets.

With fascination Jo watched as the taxi sped across a bridge from which she caught her first real glimpse of the city, with its high-rise office blocks, multi-storied buildings and flashing neon lights. Soon they headed away from the heart of the city through busy suburban streets, until they began to climb a mountain.

'See those red lights up there? They're on top of the TV towers. This is Mt Coot-tha and most of the TV channels have their studios up here,' said Mrs Patrick who, with her limited knowledge of Brisbane, had done her best to keep up a running commentary on the landmarks as they passed.

As the car snaked its way around the mountain, Jo grew more and more excited, and she began to bite her nails nervously.

'Look back down there. Isn't it beautiful?' exclaimed Mrs Patrick again, pointing through the window.

'It's unreal!' gasped Jo, as she gazed upon a panorama of fairy lights as the sprawling city of Brisbane lay spread out before her in the soft evening rain.

At the top of the mountain they passed a lookout beside a restaurant, then they headed on along a lonely stretch of road that seemed, at first glance, to lead only to bush. Jo was about to ask how much further they had to go, when they rounded a bend and she saw lighted buildings up ahead and the tall columns of the TV towers. She knew they had arrived.

'Here you are then,' the taxi driver called over his shoulder, as he drew into the kerb outside a long, brightly lit building with 'Channel 6' in large illuminated letters on the front.

'Thanks awfully, Mrs Patrick. Goodbye.' Jo muttered quickly.

'Goodbye, Jo, and good luck,' Mrs Patrick called after her, as she scrambled out.

9
Caught!

Jo STOOD AND WAVED AFTER THE taxi as it moved down the road and out of sight. Then she looked in awe at the rows of parked cars in the parking lot; a group of well-dressed people were disappearing through the glass doors into the brightly lit vestibule of the studios.

Taking a deep breath, Jo plucked up the courage to follow them but, once inside, she wished that she hadn't entered. People seemed to be hurrying about in all directions. She felt so terribly conspicuous in her grubby jeans and old peak cap. The group of people she had followed were being ushered down a royal-blue carpeted corridor by a black-suited, middle-aged man — probably the manager, Jo thought in a moment of wild panic. Almost at once she was aware of curious eyes upon her, but before she could beat a hasty retreat a tall, efficient young woman with upswept hair and enormous spectacles approached from behind an enquiry desk.

'May I help you?' she asked in carefully modulated tones.

'I . . . I was wondering if you could tell me where I might find Sonia Graham,' Jo blurted out.

'Miss Graham? She's in Make-up at the moment,' the receptionist replied, 'I'm afraid it'll be a couple of hours before you'll be able to see her. When she's finished in Make-up, it will be time for her to go on air.'

From behind the enquiry desk a telephone began to ring. The girl walked briskly back to answer it. As she did so, Jo turned and made her way back outside, but with a new spring in her step. At least her mother was in the building. That was something, she thought with a glow of satisfaction. But two hours! What on earth was she going to do till then?

Her tummy rumbled, reminding her that she had eaten nothing since her unfinished lunch so, despite the drizzling rain, she set off down the road towards the restaurant she had noticed earlier beside the lookout.

There Jo bought sandwiches and a malted milk, which she ate ravenously. As she looked at the twinkling lights of Brisbane, she rehearsed to herself how she planned, so soon now, to introduce herself to her mother.

When she returned to the studios nearly two hours later, the enquiry desk was empty, with nobody at all in evidence. Jo slipped unobtrusively down the corridor till she came to a large pair of double doors on the left-hand side, above which were the words 'Studio 1'. Above, a red light glowed and there was a sign on one of the doors that read 'Do not enter if light is red'.

There was a circular insert of glass in each of the doors and, after a quick glance over her shoulder to ensure that she wasn't being observed, Jo gingerly raised her eyes to one of them and peeped inside. The room looked much like any concert auditorium with people seated in rows facing a stage, except that on the very brightly lit stage a dozen people were seated at telephones which all seemed to be ringing at once. Other people were dashing about, apparently taking messages from one person to another, but in front of them, talking and laughing with one of the TV announcers, was her mother.

Jo's heart skipped a beat. There she was in the flesh. Jo simply couldn't believe it.

'You can't go in till the light turns green, you know,' said a voice behind her. Jo turned to find herself confronted by a man wearing an enormous Panda costume.

'I know,' she whispered, waiting for the man to ask her what business she had there but, when he didn't, her confidence returned. She wanted to shout proudly and say 'That's my mum in there,' but all she could manage was 'Who are you?'

'I am Sago the Panda,' he said with a mock salute, 'but I'm about to turn into a human being' he chuckled and turned down a side corridor.

'Whew!' breathed Jo, with relief. But when she heard a burst of laughter from the room opposite, she decided that she had better make herself scarce.

Sago had obviously gone to his dressing room. Were all the stars' rooms down that corridor? Could she find her mother's? Like some thief Jo crept cautiously down the corridor. Yes, a name was on each door. There, on her right, was a door with a strip of polished wood bearing the name 'Sonia Graham' in removable gold letters.

Jo tried the handle which responded to her touch. The next minute she was inside her mother's change room. There was a closed-circuit television set in one corner, an open wardrobe with a long black evening gown hanging inside it and a brightly-lit dressing-table with a stool in front of it.

For a moment Jo sat on the stool, lovingly fingering some brushes and combs and a gold mesh purse that littered the dressing-table. She gazed into the mirror and imagined her mother sitting there, having her hair done by one of the hairdressers. Then she scrutinised her own face in the glass. I am an ugly duckling. Why couldn't I look just a little bit like her? she thought ruefully.

Someone knocked at the door and, in a sudden panic, Jo hid in the en suite behind the door. The receptionist entered, carrying a beautiful bunch of dark red roses which she placed gently on the dressing-table. Then she left.

When she had gone, Jo crept out of her hiding-place and looked at the flowers. How wonderful to be given flowers like these! She inhaled their fragrance, admiring their delicate blooms. Oh to be really famous! she thought.

Then she jumped. Voices were approaching. They grew louder, stopping right outside the door. Once again Jo slipped behind the bathroom door, her heart pounding. Now that the moment of meeting her mother was at hand, she was gripped with real panic.

'You were brilliant, darling. And that touching speech about giving till it hurts — that was the best bit of public relations I've ever seen! You mark my words, you'll have the whole of Brisbane eating out of your hand after this,' said a man's voice. A moment later the door was thrust open and there stood her mother, smiling up at a tall, handsome man with a black moustache, whom Jo recognised from photographs to be Richard Whittaker, her mother's co-star in 'Young Executives'.

'Do you think so, Richard? Well it was really worth us coming then, wasn't it?' Jo's mother spoke in a deep husky voice that somehow surprised Jo more than anything else so far. For some reason she had expected her mother's voice to have a light musical quality. At least that had always been the way she had dreamed it would be and, ridiculously, Jo felt a little stab of disappointment.

A trolley trundled to the door and a woman's voice asked, 'Would you like a cup of tea or coffee, Miss Graham? Mr Whittaker?'

'Oh, you're an angel. I'm simply *dying* for a cup

of coffee,' Jo's mother exclaimed, as she took the cup and saucer in her hand.

'No thanks, not for me. I'm due back on air in two minutes,' replied Richard Whittaker, waving a hand in front of him. Then he bent and kissed Sonia lightly on the cheek. 'See you later, darling,' he said and he was gone.

Hastily Sonia sipped her coffee as the tea-lady said, 'I hope you don't think I'm rude, but I've just heard the news of your engagement to Mr Whittaker. I want to be one of the first to congratulate you. You'll make a wonderful couple. I'll never forget the episode of the wedding on the telly. You looked so beautiful I cried buckets.'

'Oh, that's very sweet of you.' Sonia drained her cup and handed it back to the tea-lady. 'Now I've got five minutes to get changed. Some guy's promised to give $100 if I sing one of my old night-club numbers. Singing's not really my scene any more, but in this game you soon learn to give the public what they want.'

'Oh, but Miss Graham, you sing *beautifully*!' exclaimed the tea-lady.

'Not as well as I can act, I'm afraid, but I really must fly. The hairdresser will be here in a minute to fix my hair and I must be ready for her,' replied Sonia, turning to close the door.

'See you later — and all the best,' the tea-lady called out as she trundled her trolley down the corridor.

Sonia shut the door and, humming a little tune, walked across and glanced casually at the card pinned to the flowers on the dressing-table. 'Poor old Geoff — he never stops trying,' she laughed as she carelessly pushed the roses aside and flung the card into a rubbish bin alongside the colour television, before turning to the open wardrobe.

Jo was aghast. It didn't seem right somehow to

treat a well-wisher's gift like that. Suddenly the closeness of her mother's presence made Jo feel tongue-tied. She wanted to step out and say, 'Hi Mum, I'm Jo,' but something held her back. Was it because her mother was different from what she had expected, Jo wondered in dismay, or was it because she herself was just too scared to face her?

Just then there was a tap at the door and the hairdresser, a small woman with closely cropped hair, entered the room.

'I'll only be a second,' called Sonia, as she unzipped herself, stepping out of the street-length blue chiffon frock she was wearing into the long black gown that hung in the wardrobe. A moment later she was seated at the dressing-table and the hairdresser, whose name was Tara, was deftly unpinning the formal hairstyle until Sonia's long blonde hair fell in a cascade onto her shoulders. Just when Jo was plucking up the courage to announce herself, somebody outside called 'Ready Miss Graham' and, before Jo knew what was happening, her mother, looking breathtakingly beautiful in her off-the-shoulder gown, was rushing out of the door.

As Tara turned to gather up her equipment, suddenly Jo sneezed. It came out totally unexpectedly and there was nothing that she could do to stop it. Tara raced to the door and screamed; people started coming from everywhere.

Then a dark-suited man pushed his way through.

'Oh John, he gave me such a fright. He was hiding behind there all the time I was in the room,' Tara began to explain, pointing behind the door.

'Very well, Tara. I'll handle this. That'll do everyone,' he called to the small crowd now gathered outside. 'You may go back to your duties.' The crowd melted away and he walked briskly over and looked at Jo severely.

'You, young man, come with me,' he said.

'Oh please, sir. I'm not a thief. . . or anything. And I'm not a young *man*. I'm a girl. I just wanted to see Miss Graham. Please, it really is *very* important.'

As John Brennan strode impassively along the corridor, Jo wasn't sure he had heard a word she had said. She was vaguely aware of eyes turned curiously on her from half-closed doors. Once she heard a snigger of laughter.

At the end of another corridor was a frosted glass door, with the word 'Manager' printed on it in gold lettering. Mr Brennan flung the door open and walked briskly to a polished mahogany desk, behind which stood a leather swivel chair. Without a word he sat down and turned to face Jo.

'So, you're a *girl*. Well, in any case what's the meaning of hiding yourself away in Miss Graham's private room like you did? I've a good mind to call the police,' he began.

'Please, sir, I'm not a thief. . .' Jo tried again to explain. 'I just had to see Miss Graham. It's very important. . . Actually it's a family matter.' Jo thought Mr Brennan might really think that she was stretching the truth if she told him she was Sonia Graham's daughter.

The studio manager remained unconvinced and Jo, suddenly terrified at the prospect of being thrown out into the street without even getting a chance to speak to her mother, turned to him, her lips quivering. 'Oh, please believe me, please,' she begged earnestly.

'Huh? A family matter you say? Well, that's different,' Mr Brennan began, his voice softening a little. 'Do you have any form of identification on you?'

Jo shook her head miserably. 'No, but if you mention my name to Miss Graham, she'll know it. She will, I promise.'

Mr Brennan shrugged and made a helpless gesture with his hands. 'Okay then, but you'd better be on the level. Why didn't you ask the receptionist at the desk if you could see Miss Graham? That would have saved a lot of trouble.'

'I *did* — ages ago, but there was too long to wait, so I went away. When I came back she wasn't around, so I found my way to the dressing room,' Jo said, her eyes on Mr Brennan's shiny black shoes under the desk.

'I see... well, since there is still a while to wait before Miss Graham will be finished, would you like to go and watch the show in the studio?' Mr Brennan asked with a jerk of one hand in the direction of the studio. Jo was taken aback. The last thing she wanted was to risk sharing this precious reunion with a lot of strangers.

'No... no thankyou. You see, she doesn't expect me actually. I was going to give her a surprise,' Jo replied rapidly, her tongue loosening more as her confidence grew.

Mr Brennan shook his head impatiently. 'Okay, suit yourself. I'm expecting a visitor in a moment, otherwise you could have waited here. I'll just get the receptionist to take you back to Miss Graham's room.' He reached for the phone.

'Oh, please don't bother her. I can find my own way back. It's just down the passageway and around the corner. And I promise to go straight there,' Jo butted in eagerly, anxious to avoid causing any more trouble.

'Very well then,' John Brennan's smile was quite kindly this time. 'Off you go, and I'll send a message to Miss Graham as soon as she comes off air that you are waiting to see her. Oh, er, what name will I say?'

'Jo... Jo Lacey, sir,' said Jo, pausing at the door.

'You did say *Jo*, didn't you?' Mr Brennan repeated, eyebrows raised.

'Yes, that's right.' Jo nodded, not offering any further explanations. She then turned and walked down the corridor as fast as she could, eager to cover the distance without encountering any more curious faces.

10
The Reunion

WHEN JO REACHED her mother's dressing-
room, she closed the door, breathing a loud sigh of
relief that everything was going to turn out right
after all. She went over to where her mother's frock
still lay crumpled on the floor and picked it up,
holding it against her cheek. It smelled strongly of
expensive perfume and all at once a lump rose in her
throat. She was so close now, so very close to the
realisation of her dream. Her heart beat fast with
excitement.

Holding the frock against her thin body, she sank
onto the stool in front of the mirror and looked at
herself. How pretty the dress was! It made her look
almost pretty, too! She stood up and pranced around
the room, the gold purse around her arm, imagining
herself to be the celebrated television actress. She
couldn't resist smiling at her incongruous
appearance, with the cap still perched jauntily on
her head.

Suddenly, there were female voices outside. Her
legs turning to jelly, Jo slipped behind the door of
the en suite to catch a glimpse of her mother's face
before her mother actually saw her. She was
trembling like a leaf. Her mum hadn't wasted any
time in coming. She must want to see her after all!
Would she just hug her and say, 'Oh Jo, how you've
grown!' Or would her first words be, 'Oh Jo, I'm

sorry it's been so long. But you've never been out of my thoughts, not for a minute.'

The next minute Sonia Graham, her tense face set in hard lines, stood in the doorway, closely followed by the same receptionist to whom Jo had spoken earlier in the evening.

Sonia cast a quick glance around the room and saw nobody. 'He isn't here,' she said in the same sultry voice that Jo was coming to recognise.

'Oh, but he was,' the receptionist assured her, adding 'Actually I thought it was a *she*.'

'But you said the name was Lacey, Joe Lacey? He's six feet two, fortyish . . . '

'There must be some mistake. From what I hear it's the same person who asked to see you two hours ago. And if that is the case, she was thin, had a pointed nose and was around thirteen — fourteen perhaps,' the receptionist replied bewildered.

At this remark Jo stepped forward. 'I'm over here, Miss, Miss . . . '

'Yes, that's the same kid,' the receptionist exclaimed, pointing to Jo.

'Who the heck are you? And what do you mean by getting in here to see me under false pretences?' Jo's mother exploded angrily.

'I'm terribly sorry, Miss Graham. There's obviously been a terrible mistake. I'll go and find Mr Brennan,' the receptionist put in, her face pink with embarrassment.

The moment they were alone Jo's mother closed the door, then turned to her with a withering glance. 'Who in the name of goodness, are *you*? Can't I have some privacy even in my own dressing-room? And what do you mean by using the name of my former husband to get in to see me? I could have you punished for this.'

'But my name *is* Jo Lacey, *Joanna* Lacey,' Jo cried frantically, whipping off her cap and letting her blonde hair, so like her mother's, tumble to her shoulders. 'I . . . I'm your daughter. And, Mother, I want to come and live with you now please. In Sydney. I've travelled all the way down here by myself because I read that you were to be in Brisbane for the telethon and I wanted to see you.'

The response was electric. 'You're . . . my daughter? But that's impossible! She'd only be . . . let me see, eleven, twelve . . .'

'Almost thirteen, to be exact. I'm tall for my age. I take after my dad,' Jo put in, feeling quite deflated.

'Yes, yes I can see the resemblance now.' Jo's mother had turned as white as a sheet. She stood like somebody carved out of stone, simply staring at Jo.

'He sent you, I suppose, times being hard with the drought. Well, this beats everything. I knew he'd do anything to save Tinoonan, but I never thought he'd stoop to sending you to me asking for money.'

'No, no, it's not like that,' Jo protested. 'He had nothing to do with it. It was my decision entirely. Oh, please let me stay with you. Please,' Jo begged.

'Stay with *me*? Oh, I don't know. You must give me time to think.' Her mother wiped a hand across her brow with a fluttery gesture.

'But, Mother, aren't you glad to see me? I've waited so long for this day.' Jo took a step towards her, but her mother retreated as men's voices were heard approaching.

'Look, honey, I . . . oh, my head's in a whirl. I can't do anything tonight. Come and see me in the morning and we'll talk then, eh?' she whispered rapidly.

'But . . . you mean I can't stay with you? Not even *tonight*? But I've got nowhere else to stay,' Jo blinked back a tear.

'Look, sweetie, Richard and I have just

announced our engagement. We're going on to a party with some of our television friends. I can't take you with me. The party will be going on until all hours. And you can't stay at the hotel with me — it's booked out tonight, I know that for a fact. Look, take this.' Out of the mesh purse on the dressing table she took a fifty dollar note.

'Take a cab to the Metropolitan Hotel. They're pretty good there. They'll give you a bed for the night. And come and meet me around ten... no, eleven tomorrow morning at the Tartan Coffee Lounge in the city. It's right next door to the Poinsettia Hotel where we're staying. We'll discuss the situation then. Oh, there you are, Richard, John,' she turned and in silky tones greeted the two men as they stormed into the room.

Jo stood there, stunned. She simply couldn't believe that her mother was sending her away.

'Miss Graham, I'm most terribly sorry. The girl, she lied...' John Brennan began apologetically.

'What's the trouble? Who is this?' Richard Whittaker put in, looking curiously in Jo's direction.

'Don't fuss, Richard. There's no trouble really,' Jo's mother said with a wave of her hand. 'And please don't apologise, John. It's quite okay. It's such a long time since we two met that I didn't recognise a member of my own family, but it's all sorted out now.'

'A member of the family! Aha, don't tell me — the kid sister's run away from home because she wants to follow in her big sister's footsteps. Yes, I can see a faint resemblance. It's the hair. Don't you see it too?' Richard asked the studio manager, as both men stared hard from mother to daughter.

Jo waited for her mother to put the record straight and introduce her as her daughter, not her sister. But she didn't. She simply said in honeyed tones,

70

'Richard, I'd like you to meet Joanna. Joanna, this is my fiance, Richard Whittaker, and of course you've already met John Brennan, our studio manager.'

Jo nodded to Richard and carefully avoided John Brennan's eyes.

'Well, darling, time's getting on. If you're quite ready, we'd better be getting along to the party. Everyone's waiting. Do you wish to join us, Joanna?' Richard turned courteously to Jo.

But before Jo could open her mouth to reply, her mother rushed in, 'Oh no, Joanna's just off, *aren't* you, dear?'

'Well, come on then, Sonia,' said Richard, taking Jo's mother possessively by the arm and steering her towards the door.

'If it's all right, I'll collect my things tomorrow night, John. Perhaps you would ask the receptionist to phone a cab for Joanna. It's too late for her to be out alone. And don't forget tomorrow at eleven — it's a date,' she called over her shoulder to Jo, as she and her fiance made their exit.

'After you then, Jo*anna*,' said John Brennan, emphasising the 'anna' part significantly. With a sinking heart, Jo allowed him to escort her down the passageway to the foyer.

'Just wait here,' was all he said curtly to her, indicating a chair beside an enormous potted palm as he went to speak to the receptionist. Then, bidding Jo a hasty goodnight, he bustled away as if he had much more important things to attend to.

'The cab'll be here in five minutes,' the receptionist called across to Jo, who waited pale-faced in the shadow of the palm.

'Thanks,' Jo murmured, rising to her feet and keeping her face averted. 'I think I'll wait on the steps,' and she beat a hasty retreat through the glass doors before the tears started falling in earnest. She was mad with Mr Brennan for treating her as if she had been up to some childish prank and with Richard Whittaker for whisking her mother away from her. But most of all she was mad with herself. Oh, why hadn't she spoken up the moment she had first seen her mother? Then everything would have been all right.

A pair of headlights appeared around the bend in the road and a moment later a cab pulled up alongside her. 'Miss Lacey?' the driver put his head out of the window and inquired.

Jo nodded. The taxi-driver leaned over and opened the door for her and she stumbled into the back seat.

'The Metropolitan, wasn't it?' asked the driver over his shoulder.

'Yes, please,' Jo nodded, choking back her sobs.

'Been to the telethon, eh?' he went on conversationally, but Jo didn't reply. The taxi-driver gave up attempting any further conversation until he deposited her at the door of the Metropolitan Hotel.

11
Alone

WITH LEADEN FEET JO ENTERED the lobby of the hotel. She climbed three marble stairs and found herself in a lounge, with comfortable leather chairs set around the walls and a long polished desk marked 'Reception' at one end. Her sneakers sank into the thick carpet as she walked towards the desk and gazed around.

The room had a homely atmosphere somehow and, in spite of the disappointing turn the evening had taken, Jo felt her spirits beginning to rise. All at once she realised she was dog-tired, and all she wanted to see right now was a bed where she could sleep the clock round. And then, who knew, in the morning everything might seem different. After all, she had given her mother no warning of her arrival — and it would have been embarrassing for her to have to take her, all grubby and travel-stained, to a party with her trendy friends.

Suddenly Jo was aware of a maroon-coated, bespectacled man behind the counter looking at her.

'Oh, I'm sorry. I was miles away. Could I have a room for the night, please?' Jo stammered.

'Hmmm! That could be arranged,' the gentleman opened a register. 'Would you sign here please?' and he handed it to her.

'Ahem!' the man cleared his throat. 'Would you mind my asking your age?' he went on, as Jo signed her name with a flourish.

She was tempted to say fourteen for, after all, hadn't the receptionist at the TV studios taken her for fourteen?

'Thirteen,' she whispered, turning her head away from the steady stare.

'Pardon me for saying so, but aren't you a little *young* to be booking into a room at a hotel at this late hour — alone?' the man persisted.

'Yes... yes, I guess so. But I have nowhere else to go. Oh, I can pay,' Jo added, placing her purse on the counter and showing him the fifty-dollar note.

'Just one moment, please,' replied the man, turning into an inner office and closing the door. Jo raised herself on her tiptoes and just managed to peep through a glass panel in the door. She saw that the man was telephoning somebody — probably the police. After all, there was probably some law about young girls hanging about the city alone in the early hours of the morning.

Suddenly, Jo was filled with panic. If the man was telephoning the police and if they had heard from her father reporting her as missing, then she could very soon find herself shut away in some home for delinquent girls. Nothing must be allowed to prevent her from seeing her mother tomorrow and explaining everything. She was sure that once her mother had heard the whole story, she would understand why she left Tinoonan.

Soundlessly Jo crept out of the vestibule and, once outside, she ran blindly down the street. She just wanted to put as much distance as possible between herself and the Metropolitan Hotel.

Jo paused outside a lighted sign that read 'Guest House' and wondered if here she might find accommodation for the night. It was only then that she reached in her pocket for her purse and realised that she had left it behind on the counter. A cold sense of dread overcame her.

Now she was a vagrant. Now she could, by law, be picked up by the police. Wearily she plodded on and at last found herself approaching the gates of a park by the river. Amongst the trees inside the park she could see figures walking about — and hear raucous, drunken laughter.

She turned away. The last thing she wanted to do was to become involved with some drunken party but, even as she turned away, her utter sense of loneliness overwhelmed her. Even they had their friends, her mother had Richard and all of her other trendy friends, and back at home her father had Fiona and the kids. Jo had nobody.

Slowly she retraced her steps towards the more brightly illuminated part of the city. If she could find the city square that she had passed earlier in the evening, perhaps she would be able to find a bench she could sleep on. She was so tired — so terribly, terribly tired. But try as she might, she couldn't find her way back to the square. A police car cruised towards her and she slipped into a darkened doorway. She was so weary that she was beginning to settle there for the night, when a car-load of youths drew into the kerb in front of her. With cat-calls and wolf-whistles they called out to her, one of them reaching open the car door inviting her inside.

In a panic Jo started to run and, as she did so, the car still cruised along beside her, the door held open. Jo's throat was dry and she felt as if her lungs would burst.

'Oh where is that police car now?' she whispered to herself — and then a dark figure lurched towards her from a bus shelter, pulling her inside.

'You'll be safe from them here,' a gravelly voice said to her. His breath reeked of alcohol and, terrified, Jo shook herself free from his grasp. But she was so exhausted she could do no other than collapse onto the seat, clasping her head between her knees, waiting for something dreadful to happen. But nothing did.

'There, they've gone,' the man said with satisfaction a few minutes later. 'Now, what's a kid like you doing on the streets at night,' he mumbled.

Jo was still too afraid to look at her captor but, when she heard him unwrapping a packet and a moment later smelled hot chips, she could no longer keep her head averted.

The man was, she guessed, about sixty years of age. His hair was white and although his clothes were unkempt and his shoes ill-fitting, his eyes showed kindness.

'Want some?' he said, offering her the packet.

'Oh, yes please.' Jo's mouth had begun watering and suddenly she realised she was hungry again.

'Here, have the lot.' The man passed the whole packet over to her, but she pushed it away.

'Oh no, I couldn't possibly. You see I can't pay you for them. I've lost my purse.' And, before she knew it, she was pouring out the whole story.

'Ah,' her new-found friend shook his head sadly when she had finished. 'D'ya know what I think?' He raised his bushy eyebrows but didn't wait for her to answer. 'I think you should catch the next bus back home. Yer father's likely worried sick by now.'

'But I can't. Don't you see? I've made contact with my mother now. I *can't* go back,' Jo replied quickly, munching a chip.

'Let me tell you a little story. It's about me and it's the reverse of you. You see, I had a home once and a little girl 'bout your age. Only in my case, I was the one who walked out. That were six year ago, and there's nothing I wouldn't give to see me little girl again.' The man stopped and shook his head sadly.

'Well, why don't you just go back?' Jo asked. 'After all, six years is a long time.'

To Jo's surprise, there were real tears in his eyes when he answered. 'No, I can't go back to her. Ya see she's dead,' he finished bluntly.

'Oh, I am sorry. I am... terribly sorry.' Jo knew she sounded dumb, but she didn't know what else to say. For a while an embarrassed silence hung between them.

'It was me, her dad, who let her down,' he went on, as if Jo wasn't there.

'Oh no, not really. You never stopped loving her, did you?' Jo put in gently, touching his sleeve.

'No, but what good was that when she had no way of knowing that I still cared?' He shook his head and hunched his shoulders miserably. 'So, now d'you see why you ought to go back?'

For a few minutes Jo was silent, not wanting to upset him. And then she said softly, 'But... but it's different with me. My father doesn't need me any more and I think in time my mother will.' Her voice faded away as she realised that her companion was no longer listening, but had fallen asleep, his chin resting on his chest.

Gently, Jo reached over and eased him into a more comfortable position against the wall and, as she was so desperately tired herself, she tucked her feet up on the bench alongside him and tried to go to sleep, too.

But it was no use. Every time she closed her eyes, she was tormented by the picture of those youths calling to her, almost compelling her to go with them. What if they came back?

'Er... excuse me,' Jo whispered, unsure whether or not she should disturb the man, but determined she wasn't going to spend the rest of the night in a bus shelter.

'W... what's up? The cops?' He opened his eyes and lifted his head with a jerk.

'No, no, it's only me,' Jo whispered. 'Do you

know anywhere around here where I might be able to stay free for one night? Maybe I could pay them back tomorrow. I'm scared here,' she finished with a little shiver.

'Course you are. An' so you ought to be. Now you just come with me and I'll fix you up.' He rose to his feet, his head swimming dizzily for a moment until he regained his balance. Then he set off with slow, unsteady steps. Eagerly Jo followed him.

12
Shelter

TWO BLOCKS BACK towards the river Bob halted outside an old red-brick building with the words 'Men's Refuge' written in black, faded letters across a poorly lit sign over the door. He thumped three times on the thick wooden door.

'I can't stop here. It's only for *men*,' Jo tugged at his coat-sleeve, horrified.

'You haven't much choice the way I see it, not if you don't want to be picked up,' Bob mumbled as a light was switched on inside the building. The door was opened by a middle-aged man, clad only in striped pyjama trousers.

'Bob, you old so-and-so, what do you mean by gettin' me up at this hour? I told you the last time that you had to make it in by ten, eleven at the latest,' he objected loudly.

'It's okay, it's okay, boss. It's not for me,' Bob replied, putting a hand up as if fending off a physical blow.

'As a matter of fact it's a bed for a lady I'm wanting. Do you think you could stretch a point...?'

'No, no women allowed here, Bob; you know that,' the manager of the refuge thundered.

'Aw c'mon, boss. We're mates, ain't we? Just this once, for a special favour. You see she's got nowhere to go and the coppers'll pick her up for sure or, worse still, some bloke — and she's only young...'

79

At this Bob stood aside to let the light fall full on Jo's pale, pinched face out of which her enormous eyes gazed pleadingly.

'Her! But she's only a kid! She ought to be home with her. . .'

'I know. But her home's miles away and she's got nowhere. C'mon, Mr Gould, just till the morning. She'd sleep anywhere — on the couch in the office, maybe?' Bob suggested boldly.

'Well, food's off. You're too late for that,' the other man objected, weakening.

'That's okay. We're not hungry, are we?' Bob winked across at Jo, who shook her head vigorously.

'Okay, you'd better both come in.' Mr Gould drew back for them to enter. 'But if this is just one of your schemes to get yourself in here late, I'll have your hide, you blooming scoundrel,' he said with a threatening look at Bob, as he and Jo crossed the threshold.

'It's not mate, honest,' Bob protested as he continued to walk through the hallway as if he owned the place. 'Same room as last time?' he called back over his shoulder.

'Yep. Got a full house because of the rain, but there's one empty bed in there,' Mr Gould replied, then he turned to look full at Jo's face. She was even younger than he'd at first thought. These homeless kids! Every day there were more of them. Something would have to be done, he thought to himself.

'Well, seeing you're here I'd better introduce myself. The name's Barry Gould. My wife and I run this place. What's your name?'

'Jo Lacey,' Jo replied nervously.

'Well, Jo, you haven't been ''shooting'' have you,' Mr Gould said bluntly. Her eyes didn't look like it, but sometimes one couldn't tell.

'No, I'm not allowed to shoot until I'm thirteen.

Dad always promised he'd take me 'roo shooting with him then,' Jo said in a little voice.

Mr Gould shrugged his shoulders. 'Forget it, kid. I don't mean shooting with guns. I mean heroin — drugs.'

'No, oh no. Do you have people like that here?' Jo gasped in dismay.

'Sometimes,' Mr Gould nodded. Then he jerked his head towards a room to the left of the front door. 'Okay, in there — in the office. You'll have to doss down on the couch. And not a squeak out of you, do you hear? If you cause any trouble, you'll be back out on the street so fast you won't know what hit you,' Mr Gould shook a stern finger at her.

Then suddenly he smiled. Jo thought what a pity it was that he didn't smile more often because it changed his whole face, as if a light had been switched on inside somewhere.

Just then a lady with wispy grey hair appeared in the doorway, wrapping a faded pink dressing-gown around herself. 'I thought I heard voices,' she said glancing across at Jo.

'Just another of these homeless kids turned up — a girl this time. I told her she can sleep in the office,' her husband said bluntly, adding 'I wasn't going to wake you.'

'Oh you should have, Barry. Would you like a cup of Milo, dear, or a bowl of soup?' the lady asked kindly, but Jo was past wanting anything but bed.

'No thanks, really. I'd just like to go to bed,' she replied, stifling a yawn.

'Well, off you go then. I'll just fetch you a blanket,' said the woman, going to a cupboard in the hall and taking out a thin grey blanket which she handed to Jo. 'Sleep well then, dear. Perhaps in the morning we can have a chat. Goodnight.'

'Thankyou,' murmured Jo, and then she hesitated.

'Will you be right then?' Mr Gould asked, yawning openly himself.

'Well, there is just one thing. Could you tell me where the bathroom is please?' Jo said quickly.

'Of course, dear. Take the first turn right and it's at the end of the passageway,' smiled Mrs Gould. 'I'll wait for you here.'

When Jo returned, Mr Gould was nowhere to be seen.

'Goodnight then,' Mrs Gould smiled.

With a wan smile Jo returned her 'goodnight' and hurried to the office where she climbed onto the couch and was asleep almost before her hostess had turned out the hall light.

The grey light of dawn was already infiltrating the dingy green venetian blinds when Jo awoke and, for the first time, took a good look at her surroundings. The furnishings comprised a desk and a swivel chair in one corner of the room, a filing cabinet in another, a worn green patterned carpet on the floor and, of course, the couch on which Jo had slept.

Somewhere in the building a man was calling out and cursing at no one in particular. Elsewhere there were the occasional sounds of voices and footsteps. Then she heard Mr Gould speaking to the man who had been calling out, telling him that if he didn't shut up he'd be out on his ear. She decided that if she didn't want to get involved in a lot of unwelcome questions it was time for her, too, to get out.

She opened the office door. A youngish man was just leaving by the front door. She raced after him. 'Do you know if Bob is awake yet?' she asked.

'Bob? Bob who?' the young man asked, raising his eyebrows at the sight of a girl in the place.

'Oh, I don't know his other name. Bob... he came in late last night,' she replied impatiently.

'Oh him! No, he's dead to the world. He won't be stirring for hours yet,' he said with a shrug and, abruptly turning, opened the door and walked out.

Feeling bad because she would have liked to thank Bob for all that he had done for her last night, and Mr and Mrs Gould too, for that matter, Jo followed the man, shutting the door gently after her.

Seeing a cleaner just leaving an office block, Jo asked the directions to the Tartan Coffee Lounge. Even though she knew she would have hours to wait before her appointed meeting with her mother, she began to make her way slowly there. The city didn't look nearly as frightening as it had the night before and Jo found the coffee lounge without any trouble.

Outside, there were several umbrella-covered tables and chairs, one of which Jo claimed. She was there when a girl in a white dress with tartan trimmed collar and cuffs came and opened the door at nine o'clock. The aroma of coffee that emanated from the little shop was almost more than she could bear.

Suddenly she found herself thinking about home. Fiona always had coffee for breakfast, black coffee and toast, but her father ate an enormous plate of cereal followed by a lavish helping of bacon and eggs. Jo wondered what her father was doing now and if he had missed her much. Her conscience worried her a little bit for leaving without a word, but she consoled herself that he'd get her letter today. Even if he'd been worried at first, he would stop worrying then.

13
Coming clean

IN THE CAMP HE SHARED with his grandfather down on the creekbed, Karl had also spent a
sleepless night. Not only had he missed Jo's
company during the day, but his conscience
troubled him. He should never have agreed to wait
for twenty-four hours before he spoke up. Never!

He was still silent and brooding over breakfast.
When his grandfather asked him a question, he
jumped guiltily.

'I said what's troubling you, lad? You haven't
heard a word I been saying. And it was the same
thing last night.'

'Sorry Pa', Karl flushed. 'It's just that...' he
broke off as, in the distance, he heard a faint
whinney. He had hidden Firefly in the bush,
because he was afraid that his grandfather would
have insisted that he take the horse back before the
twenty-four hours were up. This would have meant
him breaking his promise to Jo.

Just then the engine of a car was heard across the
creek, and a moment later Mr Lacey's landrover
appeared through the trees, with himself at the
wheel and a police officer riding alongside him.
Soon they were crossing the dry creekbed on foot
towards the Lofts' camp. Karl rose anxiously to
meet them, but his grandfather motioned him aside
and walked himself towards the two men.

'Sergeant Davies, Canobie Police,' said the

policeman, introducing himself. 'We're wondering whether you might be able to help us. We're looking for this girl. She seems to have disappeared. Have you seen her at all around here?' He held out a photograph of Jo.

Both Karl and his grandfather shook their heads.

'Me lad and I have only known Jo Lacey for a few days, Sergeant, and a lovely lassie she is too. But neither me grandson nor I have seen her for the past twenty-four hours and I'm afraid neither of us knows where she is.' He glanced at Karl who nodded his agreement.

'Earlier in the week she was giving me grandson here riding lessons after school, but we've not seen her or the horse since the day before yesterday. Fact is I was wondering if the kids hadn't had a bit of a scrap...'

'Don't worry, we've found the horse tethered about half a mile back there in the scrub. Suspiciously near your camp!' Mr Lacey put in quickly.

The policeman looked at Mr Lacey and shook his head.

'But you're sure you haven't seen the girl wandering about — yesterday or this morning? I mean, perhaps she's had an accident and has lost her memory... ' he persisted tactfully.

'No,' both Karl and his grandfather answered simultaneously.

'And you say she was giving you riding lessons?' Mr Lacey looked at Karl incredulously, adding, 'You know her well, then?'

Karl nodded again, then looked hurriedly down at his toes.

'What I tell you is gospel, Mr Lacey,' said Grandpa Lofts, looking Mr Lacey straight in the eye. 'She's a great girl, that one. I wouldn't lie to you about her, not me.'

For a moment Mr Lacey looked nonplussed, but something in the old man's eyes convinced him that he was telling the truth.

'Oh well, Ted, it looks like we're wasting our time. We'd better leave it there,' he sighed, and together he and the policeman walked back to the landrover and drove away.

'Well, lad,' Grandpa Lofts looked at Karl after they had gone. 'Has your glum mood got anything to do with all this?'

'Oh Pa, Pa... I don't know what to do. You see, I promised. And a promise is a promise,' Karl burst out.

'Ah, lad, but an *unwise* promise, one that is likely to cause hurt or hardship to someone else, is not a good one to make in the first place. This is where age and experience come in. You've got to learn when to be wise about making such promises,' Grandpa Lofts said gently.

'Strike, Pa! You really make me feel bad. You see, I promised when she left that I'd keep quiet for twenty-four hours. It'll soon be that now anyway,' Karl muttered, looking relieved.

'When she left? You mean she's cleared out — gone some place? And you knew all the time?' Grandpa Lofts raised his eyebrows. 'But she told me only the day I met her that she'd never leave Tinoonan.'

'Yes, yes I know. But something happened to change that,' broke in Karl, and he went on to tell his grandfather about the broken bed-lamp and about Mick Fountain blackmailing Jo.

'Well, me lad,' Grandpa Lofts said, 'There's only one thing for you to do. You go right over and tell Mr Lacey everything you've just told me.'

'Oh, but I can't... I can't! He might beat the living daylight out of me. He hates us prospectors at the best of times. When he knows I was keeping something back, he'll hate me more,' Karl said miserably.

'It was wrong of you not to tell Mr Lacey what you knew,' replied Grandpa Lofts. 'You should've told him when he was here. It seems to me there's been far too many things left unsaid already. Now Jo's gone and her father's beside himself with worry. If you're a man, now, you'll go up there and sort the whole mess out. Put his mind at rest, so to speak.'

'I don't know how you can say that, Pa, after the way he's treated you. If it was me, I'd tell him he was only getting what he deserved. I'd love to see him squirm,' said Karl, his eyes flashing in anger.

'And what would be the point of that? All I'd be doing was hurtin' meself if I did that. No, if Joe Lacey wants us out of here, then he's got the power to move us and there's nothing we can do to prevent it. But I'll go with me conscience clear, knowing that I've done the right thing. And I'll hold me head up proudly knowing that I don't hold anything against anyone.'

'Pa, you're a great guy,' said Karl, hugging the old man in a rare display of affection.

'But remember, lad, it's up to you. Like you said, you're the one who'll cop the beating, so you must decide which way you're going to play it,' Grandpa Lofts patted him on the back.

'I haven't really got much choice with someone like you around, have I? Oh well, I might as well go and get it over with. See you later, Pa,' said Karl, grabbing his hat from the tent and racing across the creek in the direction of the homestead.

'Well, what do you want?' Mr Lacey looked up from the table, where he was poring over maps of the district and discussing Jo's possible whereabouts with Sergeant Davies.

'Could I see you for a minute on your own, sir?' Karl asked tentatively.

'I'll just be outside,' the policeman said, taking the hint.

Suddenly Karl felt overawed by the large panelled dining-room, with its big family dining table and the gilt-edged paintings adorning the walls. He stood awkwardly, first on one foot and then on the other, and tried to speak.

'Well?' Jo's father waited impatiently.

Then Karl began in a rush, 'Jo's gone away to live with her mother. She's gone to meet her in Brisbane . . .'

Mr Lacey's mouth dropped open in amazement.

'Her *mother*! But she's had no contact with her since she was a baby. She can't, she mustn't . . . I mean her mother doesn't want to have anything to do with her. She mustn't be allowed to do this. It will break her heart.'

Privately Karl thought that Jo must have been nuts to think that her father didn't care. But aloud he said, 'Jo was very unhappy here and, besides, she was being blackmailed by Mick Fountain over an incident that happened a few days ago on the Pinnacle. You see she had the baby up there in the pram and it would have fallen over the cliff but . . . but for the fact that somebody was nearby and caught it.'

'And was this somebody . . . you?' Mr Lacey's face had paled at Karl's news.

'I'd rather not say, sir,' replied Karl, blushing to the roots of his hair.

'You seem to know a lot about my daughter,' Mr Lacey said, after a moment's silence. 'What is your name?'

'Karl, sir. Karl Lofts. But I haven't told you yet how Firefly came to be tethered in the scrub. You see, Jo gave her to me to look after because I can ride her, too. Only I was too scared to tell me Grandpa, so I hid her,' Karl looked down waiting for the wrath he expected, but it didn't come.

Instead Mr Lacey rose to his feet. 'Thank you for having the courage to come to me and tell me these things, Karl,' he began. Then he cleared his throat, 'and thank you for being on the Pinnacle the other day... I... please believe me, I didn't know,' he stopped, at a loss for words.

'Aw, that's okay, sir,' replied Karl quietly. 'Oh, by the way, Jo was posting you a letter explaining everything. You should get it in the mail today,' he added.

Mr Lacey passed a worried hand across his brow. 'I'm sorry to have to hustle you now, Karl, but I must get to Brisbane right away.'

Quietly Karl left the house. As he went, he heard Joe Lacey call to his wife. 'Fiona, put a few things together for me, will you? I'm driving to Brisbane right away. Jo's gone to find her mother... But before I go, I'm going to sack Fountain. He's at the bottom of this, the low-down, conniving scoundrel!'

Somewhere a baby was crying and, sitting forlornly on a swing in the garden, a little girl was saying, 'Jody gone, Jody gone,' to nobody in particular. She screwed up her little face at Karl as he went by. Not knowing how to talk to small children, he simply nodded as he walked away. But a great weight had lifted from his mind and he felt at least an inch taller.

14
Disaster

In THE DISTANCE THE CITY HALL clock was chiming eleven when Jo saw a tall, blonde young woman wearing sun-glasses and a wide-brimmed hat coming towards her from the Poinsettia Hotel. Eagerly she went forward to meet her only to turn, crestfallen, as the stranger looked beyond her and continued on her way.

A quarter-past eleven, and then half-past chimed, and still her mother did not appear. I'll give her to twelve, Jo told herself, feeling more and more disappointed as every minute passed. But when twelve o'clock came and her mother had still not put in an appearance, Jo decided to call at the Poinsettia Hotel.

Her heart was beating furiously as she entered the lobby of the high-rise, ultra-modern hotel. Silently she walked across the crimson carpet towards the flower-bedecked reception desk.

The receptionist's blonde head was bent over some papers and it wasn't until Jo cleared her throat that the girl looked up and said exasperatedly, 'Yes?'

'Er, could you please tell me the number of Sonia Graham's room? She's expecting me,' Jo added quickly. The receptionist raised her eyebrows and made a wry face. 'It's room 1202 — on the top floor.' She reached for the telephone, 'I'll tell her you're here. What is your name?'

'It's okay. Don't bother!' Jo replied, and walked quickly to the elevator. She didn't want a repeat of last night's fiasco at the studio.

She looked in dismay up at the bewilderingly intricate pattern of red and green lights and the panel of buttons above the elevator doors. But before she had time to reach out and press a button, the lift had arrived and a white-coated man asked her which floor she wanted.

'The top floor — Miss Graham,' Jo replied, hastily stepping inside. Whistling tunelessly, the liftman went about the business of pressing buttons, and soon they were whizzing up to the top of the building.

'You hoping for an autograph?' the liftman asked conversationally as he opened the door, adding, 'You'll be lucky if she gives you one. Mostly she turns kids away.'

Jo ignored the man as, with her knees knocking, she stepped out on to a plush green carpet and stared around.

'Straight across there — and good luck,' the liftman indicated a door directly in front of Jo and then began his return trip.

Her tentative knock was opened by Sonia Graham herself, dressed in a red caftan, her hair tousled as if she had just got out of bed.

'Good heavens! What time is it? I overslept,' she exclaimed languidly as she inhaled on a cigarette.

'It's ten-past-twelve,' Jo offered simply.

'It's not! How positively awful. Look, honey, I'm dreadfully sorry. Have you been waiting down there all this time?' her mother looked so genuinely sorry that Jo instantly forgave her.

'Yes,' she nodded, 'but that doesn't matter now that I've found you at last,' Jo finished with a shy flicker of a smile.

Her mother took a long look at her. 'Still, perhaps

under the circumstances, it's just as well I didn't come. I'd hate to be seen with you like *that*. You look like something the cat dragged in. What have you been doing? Sleeping in the park or something?' she asked.

Jo cast an apologetic look down at her crumpled jeans.

'Sort of. You see I lost the money you gave me, and I ended up first in a bus shelter and then in a refuge for homeless men.'

Her mother gave a little cry of dismay. 'Goodness me! That's awful! Do you realise if the police had found you sleeping in the bus shelter you could have been arrested for being exposed to grave moral danger? If that had happened, my name could have been dragged into it. Great for my career, I must say,' she finished sarcastically.

'Well, I wasn't charged and your name hasn't been dragged into it so you needn't worry,' Jo smiled apologetically and her mother's attitude at once warmed toward her.

'Well, since you're here, come and sit down and we'll talk over a cup of coffee shall we?' She ushered Jo to a seat and picked up the telephone to order the coffee.

She looked at Jo. 'You're starved, I suppose. A plate of cereal and bacon and eggs for one, thanks.' she added into the mouthpiece, and then she replaced the receiver and turned back to Jo, winding a straying strand of hair back behind her right ear.

'Now young lady, tell me about yourself,' she said, sitting on the bed and curling one leg up underneath her.

Beginning from when she could first remember, Jo told her mother about her life with her father at Tinoonan and how happy they'd been until his marriage to Fiona and how unhappy and left-out she now felt. She told her about the scene over the broken bed-lamp which had seemed the final straw, and how she could never go back, not ever.

'So you see, Mother, I've come to ask you to let me live with you from now on,' she finished, earnestly.

Her mother rose to her feet and paced up and down as she spoke.

'Sweetie, this is all a bit sudden. You see I'm at the peak of my career right now, and for me to be suddenly saddled with a teenage daughter when I'm still playing the role of a girl of twenty would be a bit of an embarrassment. Not that I don't want you, of course. There's nothing I'd like more than to have you come and live with me. But it's just not on, not right now. Besides, there's Richard. Last night we announced our engagement. He doesn't know... about you. I just don't know how he would take it if he knew he had a ready-made family...' She stopped as she saw tears welling in Jo's eyes.

'Oh, honey, it's not that I wouldn't if I *could*. But years ago I cut all ties with you... I didn't want a broken marriage and a child to interfere with my career, so I tried to pretend that those things had never happened to me. I've lived solely for my career. But I've decided I'd like to marry again. It's different with Richard because he's an actor too and he understands how I feel.' Her voice trailed away as she saw that her explanation was incomprehensible to Jo.

'Come on now, honey. Perhaps we can think of an alternative. Suppose I could get you into an exclusive boarding school in Sydney? You could come to visit me for the holidays. How would that be?' She went to Jo and placed a coaxing arm around her shoulders.

'Oh Mother, Mother,' Jo clung to her. She wanted to say, 'No, no, I want to live with you. I want you to want me as much as I do you,' but

93

meekly she nodded her head. 'I guess that'd be better than nothing,' she whispered, inwardly shuddering at the thought of a snooty Sydney boarding school compared with her carefree life at Tinoonan.

There was a knock at the door and a girl entered carrying a tray. 'Set it down there, thanks,' Jo's mother said, indicating a small round table beside the bed.

'Tuck in then, sweetie,' she went on, giving Jo a gentle push towards the food. Suddenly Jo found she had lost her appetite, but out of courtesy she forced herself to eat a little.

While Jo ate, her mother chatted conversationally about many things, occasionally quizzing her about her school work and hobbies, what she liked to eat, and what she usually did for birthday treats.

'I always thought it was beaut of you to remember my birthday every year. That's why I knew you cared about me even though you never wrote,' Jo said suddenly.

Her mother's lips tightened for a minute. 'Really?' she said and raised her eyebrows.

'What did your father say when you told him you were coming to me?' she went on, changing the subject.

'He doesn't know... ' Jo broke off suddenly.

'Doesn't know! You mean you didn't tell him? That you just ran off? Honey, he'll be frantic!' She reached for the telephone. 'I'm going to 'phone him right away. I'll tell him you're with me, and that I'm taking you back to Sydney with me next week, to school. Only for now you'll have to come as my sister, see, because that's what Richard thinks you are.'

'Get me... what's the number of Tinoonan?' she turned to Jo.

'Canobie 48,' Jo said faintly.

Just then the switchgirl's voice came on the other end of the line. 'There's an incoming call for you, Miss Graham. Will you take it first?'

'Yes, put it through,' Jo's mother said briskly. 'Hello, yes, this is Sonia Graham speaking.' There was a deathly silence and then she exclaimed, 'He's what?' There was another devastating pause and Jo sensed that the call had something to do with her. Her apprehension mounted as she heard her mother ask, 'Is he badly hurt... will he be all right?'

Again that exasperating silence. Surely it can't concern me, thought Jo to herself. It must be connected with her mother's Richard. With a sneaking sense of relief Jo waited on her mother's every word. With Richard Whittaker out of the picture, she stood a better chance of establishing a normal relationship with her mother. But just as quickly as the thought had arisen, Jo dismissed it. What sort of a girl was she becoming? Sneaky, a liar — completely self-centred?

At last her mother replaced the receiver and looked at Jo. Her face was deathly pale and her hand shook a little as she said, 'There's been a terrible accident, somewhere on the Warrego Highway. Your father's... terribly hurt. They're rushing him by ambulance to hospital down here. That was Fiona on the phone. She said she'd meet you at the hospital at two o'clock. There's only one thing that your father wants and that's to see you. You see, he was hurrying here to be with you when we met. Fiona says he was afraid you might be upset.'

Jo's legs went to jelly and she stuffed her handkerchief into her mouth and bit on it to prevent herself from breaking down completely as she slumped into her chair.

'Oh Mother, Mother, it's all my fault,' she said as her mother came to her and gathered her into her arms.

'Hush, there's no use going on about it now. But I'll get dressed and come with you to the hospital. You do want me to, don't you?' she added, as Jo shook her head.

'No, no, I can't see him. I can't. Not like that! Not knowing I'm the cause of it all. And I can never face Fiona again. Take me away now, Mother, please. *Please.*' Jo pleaded and clutched at her mother's hand.

'Would you really run away again?' her mother asked quietly. 'Sweetie, you've got to face it. What if he died not knowing that you really cared — because I can see that you do.'

Suddenly Jo remembered Bob of the night before and his despairing words about his little girl dying without knowing that he still loved her.

'Yes, of course I'll go,' Jo said at last, choking back her sobs.

Just then the door opened and Richard Whittaker walked into the room.

'Come on, Sonia, we'll be late for the radio interview. I've got a car waiting downstairs,' he said, his irritation increasing at the sight of his fiancee's kid sister who was still making a nuisance of herself.

'Oh gosh, honey, give them my apologies. Tell them I'm sick or something. I can't come, not until after two. Tell them anything. But just leave me alone for an hour or so, will you?'

Jo looked at her mother in grateful amazement. For once, for once in her life, her mother had put her first.

'Well, if that's the way you want it, so be it,' Richard stormed angrily out of the room.

'Oh dear, now look what I've done,' Jo wiped a worried hand across her brow and looked nervously at her mother.

'Don't worry, he'll be back,' her mother shrugged

confidently. 'Anyway we'd better get you tidied up and order a taxi so that we're at the hospital when your father arrives. Come on now. Then I'll organise a room for you here for a few nights until we can decide on a suitable school in Sydney where they're prepared to take you at short notice.'

Dazedly Jo got to her feet and mechanically went about the task of sprucing herself up.

This time, as she was whizzed around the city in a taxi, she scarcely saw anything. All she was aware of was a terrible sick feeling in the pit of her stomach. All she could think of was, 'What if my Dad should die because of me? Dad, Dad, I love you. Oh please God, please save my Dad.'

From the depths of her misery the prayer was uttered. She'd never been one for praying. In fact she'd never given God too much thought in her life before except, as she'd told Karl and his grandpa, to blame him for letting her mother go.

'Here we are then,' her mother said, as the driver slipped into the kerb and jumped out to open the door.

'Isn't it a big place?' Jo gazed up at the huge hospital, wondering behind which of the many windows her father lay.

Her mother said, 'There's somebody beckoning you over there.'

Jo's eyes followed her mother's pointing finger and in the distance she saw Fiona running towards her.

'Wait, I'll come with you, Joanna,' her mother called, but Jo didn't hear her. Soon she was in Fiona's arms and they were both talking at once. 'How is he?' Jo whispered.

Fiona blinked back a tear. 'Conscious. He's asking for you — come on,' she said. Blindly Jo followed her, forgetting her mother in the waiting taxi.

'Oh well, it would never have worked out,' Sonia Graham sighed a heartfelt sigh and blew her nose hard. 'To radio station 4AU please, and hurry,' she said to the driver in a controlled voice and the taxi sped away to be lost a moment later in the seething mass of traffic.

15
Reconciled

'HOW DID IT HAPPEN' Jo asked as she panted behind Fiona.

'He was speeding I guess and he took a risk that didn't come off. He wanted to reach you before you met up with... with your mother. You see, when she left she told him she wanted to forget about your existence,' Fiona said matter-of-factly as they stood before the elevator.

'But... but how could she have said *that*? All those birthday cards...' Jo stammered.

'Oh, those! I told your father it'd get him into trouble in the end,' Fiona said disgustedly.

'You mean that he organised someone to send those cards all those years, under her name? I... I don't believe it,' Jo spluttered.

'Well, he did. He got your Aunt Sara, who was an air hostess and moved around a lot, to send them from all over the place. He knew how much store you set by having a mother, so he started doing it when you were very little. Then, once he'd started it, he couldn't stop because he knew how hurt you'd be. So he just hoped you'd never find out.' Fiona stepped ahead of Jo into the lift, a crowd pressing in beside them.

'No wonder she looked a bit funny when I mentioned them,' Jo muttered into the man's back in front of her.

'You've arranged something with her, then?' Fiona asked.

'Hmm,' mumbled Jo.

'Oh,' Fiona looked grim and said no more.

The lift doors opened and Fiona and Jo pushed their way out.

'He's in here,' Fiona said, pushing open a swing door that led to a glossily polished corridor, with rooms opening off to each side.

'This one,' Fiona said stopping outside the first on the left. 'Just remember, he's very sick,' she whispered with a break in her voice. Then, turning to a nurse, 'Is it all right for us to go in?'

'Certainly Mrs Lacey. Just don't stay long and tire him,' she said with a warm smile.

Jo was dismayed to see her father's face almost as white as the bandages that swathed his head. His eyes were closed, but as Jo crept alongside the bed, he opened them and spoke her name.

'Dad! Daddy! I'm so sorry.' Jo felt the words almost choke her.

'It's... it's all right, Jo,' he breathed and his lips tried to smile, but it was obvious he was in great pain.

'Oh Dad, I love you so. Get better please.' Jo's tears were falling fast on to their clasped hands.

'I'm sorry, dear, but that's all for today,' the nurse put in from the doorway.

Jo bent to kiss her father's forehead. 'Hang in there, Dad. I'll be back later,' she whispered.

'That's my girl,' Mr Lacey smiled weakly and then sighed. 'I'm a little tired just now. I think I'll have a sleep.'

Silently Jo tiptoed away and left Fiona to say goodbye to him alone.

For two days Joe Lacey hovered between life and death, and during that time neither Fiona nor Jo left the hospital for more than a few minutes, snatching a couple of hours' sleep in the visitors' waiting room when they were too tired to keep their eyes open any longer.

On the morning of the third day the doctor told Fiona that he was going to be all right, that the danger period had passed. Jo and Fiona fell into each other's arms with joy, Jo begging Fiona, who was on the point of exhaustion, to go and get some sleep while she stayed with her father.

Reluctantly Fiona went. As Jo watched her father's gaunt face stirring in his sleep she knew, for the first time in her life, that somewhere, somehow there had to be a God. And that it was he who had given her father back to her.

At last the eyelids fluttered open and Joe Lacey looked at his daughter.

'You okay, partner?' he asked through dry lips.

With a lump in her throat Jo nodded. 'Yes, dad,' Jo gave a thumbs-up sign.

'How did you find her? Was she kind to you?' he breathed, wetting his lips with his tongue as he spoke with an effort.

'Who? My mum?' Jo leaned close.

Her father nodded. 'Was she . . . was she pleased to see you?' he broke off.

'Sshh Daddy, you mustn't talk too much. No, she wasn't pleased at first, but later,' Jo made a face, 'she changed a bit. She actually has said I could go to school in Sydney and live with her in the holidays,' Jo whispered.

'Really!' her father looked surprised. 'So it's all arranged then,' and he waved one hand in a helpless gesture.

'No, Dad. I'm going to 'phone her and tell her it's not on now. She's been telephoning the hospital every day to find out how you are. But I've made up my mind that, now that you're going to be okay, I'm going home. Fiona tells me that Mrs Banks is minding the kids. She could probably do with a hand and, besides, someone has got to get the planting started. With you and Fred McIntosh both out of action and Fountain gone, that only leaves me.'

A smile of relief passed across Joe Lacey's face. 'You really mean that, Jo? I mean, that you want to go home?'

'Yes, Dad. I've been a stupid, selfish, deceitful fool and if I hadn't been like that you wouldn't be lying here today. It's a wonder you don't hate me,' Jo lowered her eyes from her father's steady gaze.

Tenderly he reached up and cupped her cheek in his hand.

'I could never do that, my Jo,' he whispered. 'That's all water under the bridge now and probably I was just as much at fault as you were for not realising how left out you felt. Let's just call it quits and start afresh, shall we, partner?' he winked.

'Sure, boss,' Jo replied in the same vein, and it was as if the months had rolled back and they were mates again.

For a moment Mr Lacey closed his eyes, his hand clasped in Jo's. 'How do you figure on getting the planting done by yourself?' he asked suddenly, pointing out, 'After all, you've got to go to school as well.'

'Oh, I have in mind a couple of friends who might help,' Jo replied evasively.

'The Lofts?' her father asked.

Jo nodded. 'You don't mind, do you, Dad?' she hastened to add, 'They really are beaut people.'

Her father shook his head. 'I know they're your friends, Jo. But they're prospectors, not farmers,' he protested mildly.

'But Dad, I know what to do. It's just that I'll need someone to help me with the machinery,' Jo butted in eagerly.

Her father still looked doubtful.

'Well, if they're not interested or if they've moved on already I'll think of someone else. One of the Banks boys maybe,' Jo said flatly.

She was silent for a moment, and then, 'Dad, in any case if the Lofts are still there, please may I tell them that they may stay on until you come home. Please?' Jo put the delicate question gently, adding, 'We really do owe them a lot.'

'Jo, what can I say when you put it like that?' her father sighed. 'Okay, till I get back,' her father agreed with a resigned laugh. 'And now, Joanna Lacey, I hereby appoint you in charge of the outside work at Tinoonan until my return. It's up to you to decide who you want to help you, but, remember, if anyone makes a mess of things you will be responsible.'

'Thanks, Dad. Thanks,' Jo beamed.

A white-clad figure came swishing into the room in a businesslike fashion. 'Feeling a little better this afternoon, Mr Lacey?' the sister said breezily and Jo, after stooping to kiss her father goodbye, went in search of Fiona to tell her that she was ready to catch the next bus home.

16
Home again

OUTSIDE, JO FOUND FIONA deep in conversation with a smart woman in her early forties. Her grey-streaked black hair was in a french plait and she was dressed elegantly in a mauve suit.

'Jo, I don't believe you've met your Aunt Sara — your father's only sister,' Fiona said, putting a hand on Jo's arm.

Jo stared at her aunt as Fiona went on, 'She's just retired from being an air hostess, travelling all around the country, and has bought a unit at the Gold Coast.'

'So you're the one who sent me all those phoney birthday cards!' Jo said bluntly.

Her aunt smiled, a twinkling sort of smile that reminded Jo instantly of her father, and at once Jo was sorry for what she had said.

'I'm afraid so. I told your father right at the beginning that it was wrong — that you'd find out one day — but I'm afraid he was so determined that you should have a mother, in name at least, that I eventually gave in to his request. It seemed such a little thing to do at the time, if it was going to bring you happiness. Only I never dreamed that it would have led you...'

'To run away,' Jo finished flatly for her.

'I'm sorry, Jo,' Aunt Sara said and smiled again.

Jo shrugged. 'It's okay. All kids have to learn

sooner or later that there's no Santa. It's really no different to me finding out about this, is it?' she finished flippantly to hide the hurt she still felt inside.

'In case you're wondering why I'm here,' Aunt Sara continued, 'I've come to offer your father and Fiona any help I can. Goodness knows, I've been little enough help up until now. I haven't even been home to Tinoonan for a visit since I started flying twenty years ago.'

'Your Aunt Sara has very kindly offered to take you back home so that between you you may relieve Mrs Banks of the responsibility of the two girls until your father and I can get back,' Fiona put in.

'That's fine by me. I was just telling Dad that, since he's laid up as well as Fred, I'd better get back to begin the planting. I hear they've had a bit of rain,' Jo said confidently.

Fiona looked relieved. She had expected Jo to raise all sorts of objections to being sent home. 'Well, it doesn't matter to me so much about the planting as it does that we don't impose on Mrs Banks' kindness any longer than necessary.'

'And you really feel you can trust me with the girls?' Jo looked her straight in the eye.

Fiona nodded. 'Jo, you've changed this past week. I *know* I can.' She paused, then went on, 'But tell me, just how do you think you're going to get the planting done alone? It's too big a task for a young girl.'

'Just you leave that to me,' Jo said evasively. 'Dad said I could employ help if necessary and he's appointed me in charge,' she went on proudly.

'Jo, not Karl and his grandfather!' Fiona exploded. 'Really, Jo, what do they know about planting wheat? Besides, they don't come to us with any credentials. I mean, what do you really know about them?'

105

'Only that Karl saved Claire's life,' Jo said pointedly and Fiona, knowing she was beaten for the moment, left it at that.

It was six thirty in the evening when Aunt Sara turned the nose of her little Toyota car into the white painted gateway of Tinoonan station.

'Please stop the car a minute, Auntie,' Jo looked at her pleadingly and, with an indulgent smile, Aunt Sara did as she was asked.

A moment later Jo had sprung out of the car and was kneeling on the ground kissing it. 'Are you crazy? Do you want to be bitten on the lips by a bull ant?' Aunt Sara laughed and Jo, her face radiant, joined in as she rose to her feet.

'Oh Auntie, it's just so good to be home,' she said shaking her head. 'I feel as if I've been away for six weeks and yet it's only six days. I don't ever want to leave this place again,' she finished, with a spread of her hands towards the rolling acres.

'Well, for my part, I don't know what you see in the place. As a girl I couldn't wait to get away and see a bit of life,' said Aunt Sara, stepping out of the car. 'Look at it. Same old dusty brown dirt; same old scrub; same old house, no doubt, around the bend there. By day the same roasting heat and flies and, down there, the same old Pinnacle dominating the landscape . . .'

Jo flinched at the mention of the Pinnacle, but Aunt Sara failed to notice as she inhaled deeply, drawing the sharp evening air into her nostrils and filling her lungs with clear, unpolluted air. Yes, she had to admit it was invigorating. She called herself a realist and had no time for silly romantic notions, but now that she was here, there was something special about Tinoonan — something that had escaped her notice when she had been Jo's age. In a way she now envied Jo who, after less than one short week away, knew what she wanted from life, whereas she herself had spent years searching for the happiness that seemed to elude her.

'Well, young lady, are we going to stand here all night talking, or are we going up to the house to get some of Mrs Banks' good tucker? I could sure do with a bite to eat.' Aunt Sara roused herself from her reverie and strode towards the car. Jo was beside her in a flash.

'It's all systems ''go'' for the last lap of the journey, Captain,' she said, making a mock salute, and Aunt Sara turned the key in the ignition and the engine throbbed into life.

As they rounded the bend in the track they saw at once that the homestead was a blaze of lights. A toot on the horn brought Mrs Banks running out to greet them, and a moment later they were being hugged and kissed and welcomed home as if they were long-lost daughters. As indeed, in a way, they both were.

There was a movement at the door and, over Mrs Banks' shoulder, Jo caught sight of Patti peeping shyly through the crack in the door.

'I can see you, you little minx!' Jo made a dive towards her, but Patti drew back, her wide brown eyes saucers of fear.

'She's been waiting up to see you, poor lamb, and now she's all overcome,' Mrs Banks explained. But Jo knew that it was more than that. Patti's eyes reflected the fear she had felt when she had seen Jo's arm upraised hitting her and screaming at her.

'Patti, little Patti, it's Jody. I've come back. I'm not going to hurt you,' Jo called to her gently, kneeling on the floor with both hands outstretched.

The little girl gazed solemnly at her for a moment and then, springing to her feet, Jo said, 'Come with me.' Hesitatingly, Patti followed as Jo strode off in the direction of her bedroom. On her bed sat her ancient teddy bear which, like the bedlamp, had always been taboo to Patti.

'Here Patti, it's for you. To make up for... the last time...'

Slowly Patti took hold of the teddy bear and a moment later she was crushed in Jo's arms.

'I've missed you. I've missed you,' Jo whispered over and over, while Patti beamed happily at Aunt Sara and Mrs Banks who had followed silently to the doorway.

'Jody's back now. Jody's back,' she said with shining eyes.

'Yes, and this, Patti, is your Aunt Sara. She used to be an air hostess and has travelled all over Australia.' Jo made the motion of a plane flying with her hands while Patti eyed her newfound aunt with a nonchalant expression, then turned ecstatically back to the teddy bear.

'Teddy's mine now, Jody?' she asked incredulously.

'Well, look at that! She's more interested in a ragged old teddy than in her new aunty,' Mrs Banks exclaimed, laughing.

Jo looked Patti in the eye, ignoring Mrs Banks. 'Yes, Patti, he's yours now,' she whispered.

'For ever and ever?' Patti went on still unconvinced.

'For ever and ever. And now I think Mrs Banks and Aunt Sara would like you to get into bed.' Gently Jo gathered the little girl up in her arms and carried her to her bedroom and put her to bed.

'Goodnight, Patti darling. Oh, it's so good to be home,' Jo whispered as she kissed her little sister and tucked her in.

'Goodnight Jody,' Patti smiled ecstatically and hugged the teddy.

On her way out Jo paused and looked at the sleeping Claire. Stooping over the cot she kissed her on the cheek, then tiptoed out to join Aunt Sara and Mrs Banks.

17
Prowlers

'WELL I'LL BE OFF NOW, MISS LACEY,' Mrs Banks said when, after tea, she had returned from putting the last of her things together.

'Are you sure you wouldn't rather stay till morning? Do you have far to go?' Aunt Sara asked.

'Oh no, not far. About twenty kilometres or so. We're next door on the old O'Brien place. It's only twelve kilometres as the crow flies,' plump Mrs Banks said laughingly. 'Thanks, but no, I've told my crew I'll be back tonight — though I hate to think what sort of a mess I'll find the place in. Four sons I've got, and none of them house-trained as you might say.' Again she laughed at her own joke, and Aunt Sara joined in uncertainly.

'Well thanks awfully for all you've done, looking after the kids and everything,' said Jo, remembering her manners as the eldest daughter of the house.

'Don't mention it, love,' Mrs Banks pinched her gently on the cheek. 'Only glad to see you back home and in one piece.'

'Yes. . . er, my brother and his wife do appreciate all that you've done. It's wonderful to have such good neighbours,' Aunt Sara added her official thanks.

'It's been a pleasure, love. I only hope Joe will make a quick recovery and be back here in no time. Oh, by the way, I wasn't going to mention this for fear it put the wind up you both, but on second thoughts, I'd better. A couple of bikie-looking chaps wearing leather jackets with dragons on the back turned up today. Looking for Fountain, they were. They didn't believe me when I told them Fountain'd been gone for five days and, thinking I was Mrs Lacey, they demanded that I let them into the cottage to see for themselves if his stuff was there. When I refused and told them they had no business prowling around the place demanding things, they turned a bit nasty and threatened to break in anyway. I told them that if they didn't leave I'd call the police. I knew it was useless phoning my Alf or the boys to come over, because they'd all be down at the yards.'

'They got a bit threatening. You'll be sorry, they said. Nobody gets in the way of the Dragons, one of them called out. But I could see they were all bluff. Sure enough, while I was inside on the 'phone I heard them revving up their bikes and, when I came outside again, they were halfway down the track.'

'I hope they don't decide to come back,' breathed Aunt Sara when she had finished.

'They won't,' Mrs Banks assured her confidently. 'I've met their type before. Anyway, if they so much as set a foot in here again, you ring us straightaway. Alf and the boys'll be over in a flash. And if there's anything else you want, don't hesitate to give us a call.' With these words Mrs Banks walked over to her Commodore and, after slinging her port in the boot, opened the door and climbed in. A moment later she was whizzing away down the track.

Aunt Sara and Jo watched until the red glow of the car's tail-lights snaked out of sight. Then, with a sigh of nostalgia, Aunt Sara turned and looked around at the buildings. 'It's all the same except, of course, that there's nobody occupying the men's quarters now,' she sighed, as her eyes took in the

110

black shape of the cottage that had always, in her day, housed several station-hands.

'No,' Jo put in quietly, her heart beating faster at the thought of Fountain. She didn't know how much of her story Aunt Sara knew, but didn't at the moment feel obliged to talk about it.

'I'd forgotten how quiet it is. After being surrounded by people for years, it's a bit creepy to think that your nearest neighbours are twenty kilometres away,' Aunt Sara went on, with a slight shiver.

'Oh, but they're not,' Jo shrugged carelessly. 'My friend, Karl Lofts, and his grandfather are camped down on the creek. At least I expect they're still there. Dad had told them they had ten days to get out because he's got a big 'thing' about prospectors, but...'

'Prospectors! That's always been a dirty word around here,' Aunt Sara put in with a wry grin.

'Not any more, I think,' Jo put in quickly and she told Aunt Sara about the part Karl had played in saving Claire's life that day on the Pinnacle.

'Yes, I've heard about that. But you can hardly class a couple of penniless itinerant prospectors as respectable neighbours like the Banks,' Aunt Sara objected gently.

'Well, I do,' Jo put in staunchly.

'Well, you're very naive and trusting, my dear,' Aunt Sara said, giving Jo a playful push, adding, 'You forget that I've been around and seen a lot of the world.'

Jo shrugged and said nothing. After all she didn't want to get into an argument with her new adored aunty.

'Well, I, for one, have had it,' said Aunt Sara, stifling a yawn as they turned and started to walk back towards the house together.

'You go and take your shower. I think I'll sit here

for a minute,' said Jo, settling herself on the back steps and looking up at the star-spangled sky.

'It's funny, but you don't see the stars like this down in the city, do you?' she called out, but her aunt was already running the water for her shower and didn't hear her.

Jo turned her eyes in the direction of the Pinnacle, behind which was the creek and the Lofts' camp. Her father had told her how Karl had come to him and confessed that he knew her whereabouts. Her father had also told her what a fine young man Karl was. Jo could hardly wait to tell him so tomorrow, nor to tell him that he and his grandfather could stay a while longer. She also wondered if they would accept the job she planned to offer them for, despite what Aunt Sara had said about them not being respectable, she still planned to offer it. She wondered how Karl would go at driving the small tractor. Not very good, she fancied, but he'd soon learn, if his quickness to master horseriding was anything to go by.

From the direction of the stables she heard a familiar whinny.

'That sounded like Firefly,' she gasped, stepping inside for a torch, then running to the stables.

As Jo entered she was vaguely aware of a strange aroma, but in her excitement at seeing Firefly again she didn't give it a second thought.

Both the filly and King seemed jumpy and reared when they first saw her. Gently, however, Jo approached Firefly and talking softly to her gradually calmed her until she was quiet enough for Jo to fling her arms about her neck and hug her.

Firefly whinnied again, this time with pleasure.

'Jo! Where are you?' At her aunt's call Jo gave Firefly one last hurried pat, turned to King's stall and patted him also, then ran to the house.

'I was just saying "Hello" to my horse. When I

112

went away I gave her to Karl, but his grandfather must have made him bring her back, because she's in the stables. Did Mrs Banks mention anything to you about it?' she finished, with a puzzled frown.

'No, she didn't. And I'd say you're very lucky Karl's grandfather had enough decency not to allow him to keep such an expensive gift,' Aunt Sara said firmly.

Suddenly, remembering that her aunt had once been a country girl Jo asked, 'Can you ride, Auntie?'

'Sure, I'm pretty good! I'll show you one day,' Aunt Sara laughed and then yawned. 'Well, I'm for bed. Goodnight, Jo.'

'Night-night, Aunt Sara,' Jo kissed her cheek, then impulsively she threw her arms about her neck. 'Gee, it's good to have you here. Perhaps if I'd known you before none of what's happened would have happened.'

'Perhaps, Jo, perhaps...' Aunt Sara kissed her gently back. 'But who knows? You might have just looked upon me as your old-maidish aunt.'

'No way!' Jo retorted in disgust. 'I can't see you sitting in your rocking-chair knitting!'

'The time'll come soon enough, don't you worry,' Aunt Sara laughed wryly, adding, 'But right now I really am going to bed.'

'Goodnight then. I hope you sleep well,' Jo called out, and went to get her shower and make preparations for bed.

As Jo looked around her room at the empty space where her mother's bedlamp used to be, and the neatly made bed that looked so sadly incomplete without her old teddy bear, she sighed. What a long way she had come since Thursday morning when she had left to follow her dream!

She thought of Mrs Patrick up near Cairns and of old Bob. She wondered if he was at the Refuge

113

tonight, or alone wandering the streets with nobody to really care whether he lived or died. She thought of her own father. How lucky she was to have somebody who cared for her as much as she now knew that he did. She thought of her mother: glamorous, successful, but living in a world in which Joanna Lacey had no part. She did not feel bitter — a little confused perhaps, and even a little relieved that at least now she could picture her mother as a real person and not a fantasy.

Before she could go to bed, however, there was something that Jo felt had to be done. Determinedly, she went to the wardrobe and took out her scrapbook. Taking a pair of scissors, she carefully removed all of the phoney birthday cards one by one and threw them into the wastepaper basket beside her desk. Tomorrow she would burn them for she had no need of them any more. Having done this, she climbed into bed and a few minutes later was fast asleep.

18
Fire!

IT WAS THE DOGS who disturbed her. It was about ten o'clock and they were barking furiously.

'Oh lie down, Rastus and Paddy,' she moaned as she turned on to her other side and tried to get back to sleep. But the barking went on. They're probably only after a hare or a bandicoot, thought Jo sleepily, and then she heard the horses whinny and she stiffened. Something had unsettled the horses, too. That couldn't be a hare or a bandicoot!

It was then that she smelled something burning. She sat upright in bed and sniffed. There it was again, stronger this time — the unmistakable smell of smoke. Throwing back the covers she raced to the windows and saw, to her horror, that the sky to the back of the house in the direction of the stables was lit with a terrible orange glow.

'Firefly! King!' she screamed, as she raced out of the back door and around to where the garden hose was attached to the tank. Madly she tugged until it would reach no further. Then, in despair, she dropped it and ran to fill a bucket with water. A hessian bag hung over a fence near the tank-stand. She grabbed this and doused it with water then, throwing it over her head like a hood, she ran and unlatched the door of the stables. The heat leapt out at her, almost taking her breath away. Again the horses whinnied, this time frenziedly, their hooves pounding the floor as they reared in terror. As Jo opened the door to the filly's stall Firefly reared again, her front hooves almost hitting Jo on the head as she reached for her. Jo went to King's stall and released him, then made another dash toward the filly, this time grasping her by the mane and leading her out into the corral where she circled a few times before taking off at a gallop in the wake of King, through the open gate and down towards the dam.

'Get the hose connected to the tank beside the cottage, quick! It's spreading toward the barn!' Jo looked around to see Aunt Sara in her dressing-gown, her hair dishevelled, struggling towards her carrying a heavy bucket of water in each hand.

Jo's eyes flashed towards a trail of flames between the stables and the barn which was stacked with the hay for sheep fodder. It represented hundreds of dollars to her father.

With trembling fingers she soon had the hose transferred from the house tank to the cottage tank and she turned on the tap. The pressure wasn't good, but at least the hose reached. As Jo poured the steady trickle of water on to the flaming grass between the stables and the barn, Aunt Sara emptied her buckets of water on to the dry grass in a circle around the stables to prevent the fire from spreading.

'Here, I can run faster than you. You hold the hose and I'll do that,' Jo called to her Aunt Sara who, having wrenched her ankle in a hole, gratefully exchanged her buckets for the hose. Jo tore away, to return a few seconds later with two more buckets full of water which she poured onto the flames. Continuing in this fashion, they soon had eradicated any danger of the fire spreading, but the stables were completely demolished. There was nothing they could do but let them burn.

At last the fire was out and Jo and Aunt Sara

collapsed exhausted onto a couple of empty upturned petrol drums.

'I wonder how that little lot got started,' Jo said wearily as she pushed back her straggling hair and surveyed the ruins. 'It's a terrible thing to say, but I think it must have been deliberately lit,' she went on, when Aunt Sara made no comment.

'Well I'm sure it was,' Aunt Sara put in evenly, 'because on my way across here from the house I just caught a glimpse of a figure running away from the back of the barn. It was dark, of course, and I couldn't be sure whether it was male or female. But I am certain of one thing. Whoever it was, was young and agile because he ran like the wind... down that way,' and Aunt Sara jerked her head in the direction of the creek.

'Aunt Sara, you're not suggesting that Karl had anything to do with the fire! He just wouldn't do that! He loves Firefly as much as I do. He'd never do anything to harm her,' exclaimed Jo hotly.

'But your father does want them away from the place, doesn't he? And they don't want to go. I mean... they might have had it in for him,' Aunt Sara persisted.

'Yes... yes, Dad did want them to go... but Aunt Sara you've got it all wrong,' Jo insisted.

'Well what other reason could the boy have had for being here tonight?' Aunt Sara asked gently.

For a moment Jo was nonplussed. 'I don't know. I really don't. Maybe he saw the fire in the distance and came to get a closer look. Or maybe he came to see if Firefly was okay. All I know is that he wouldn't have lit the fire. Can't you understand?'

'I understand what my father thought of those types of people — and your father is just the same. They're bad news, Jo, they have no roots. They don't really belong on the land. They're... parasites. Both your father and Fiona warned me to

117

keep my eye on them,' went on Aunt Sara relentlessly.

'Oh stop it! How ungrateful you all are!' Jo stood up and ran to the fence and buried her head in her hands. 'I won't hear you, or them, say a bad word against either of the Lofts. I won't. Anyhow, what about those two bikies who came here today? They threatened Mrs Banks they'd be back. They could have started the fire, and it could be one of them that you saw running away,' Jo burst out.

'But Jo, we'd have heard them,' Aunt Sara pointed out reasonably.

'Not if they left their bikes somewhere and walked in,' Jo returned heatedly.

'Come off it, Jo. Have you ever heard of bikies walking anywhere?' said Aunt Sara gently. 'Besides, Mrs Banks was sure they were bluffing. But let's say no more about it tonight. I'm tired and I'm sure you are. Let's go and have a cup of tea and then call it a day, or rather a night — for the second time,' Aunt Sara gave a brittle laugh.

The next morning Aunt Sara tried to be bright and cheerful, but Jo could not catch her mood. She couldn't forgive Aunt Sara for the awful things she had said. Over breakfast the telephone rang and she heard Aunt Sara telling Mrs Banks all about the fire and that she suspected the prospectors of starting it. From the tone of the conversation, Jo could hear, Mrs Banks seemed inclined to agree with her.

At last Aunt Sara replaced the receiver and returned to the table. ' Mrs Banks said that her son, John, went to the movies last night and he saw the Dragons leaving the cinema. That was after 10.30. They could hardly have got back here and started the fire. It was well alight by then, as you know. So that seems to put paid to your theory about them having started the fire.' Aunt Sara paused for a moment.

Stubbornly Jo rushed in, 'But if you knew John, he's awfully vague. He could easily have been mistaken about the time.'

'Well,' went on Aunt Sara evenly, 'Mrs Banks also told me that the boy, what's his name, Karl, brought Firefly back yesterday about four o'clock. He didn't speak to her. She thought it was a bit strange that he should just dump the horse and run.' Aunt Sara gently tapped her boiled egg. Then she went on, 'Jo, I agree with her. I think he brought Firefly back so that everything would look to be on the level and then sneaked back last night and set fire to the stables, intending it to spread to the barn and goodness knows what else. I mean, dear, you think that you know these people, but how well do you really know them? Why, you only knew them for less than a week . . .'

'No, no, you're wrong, Aunt Sara.' Jo pounded the table with her spoon, so much so that Patti looked at her round-eyed and Claire began to cry. 'You shouldn't say such terrible things. I'm going right now to get Karl to come up here and tell you it's all lies,' and with that Jo leapt up from the table and stormed out of the back door.

Firefly and King were both back in the horse paddock when she went outside and gently Jo called Firefly over. Her saddle was a ruined, sodden mess, so Jo simply slipped a bridle over the filly's head and rode bare-back towards the Lofts' camp. She'd show everyone how wrong they were. She'd show them!.

'Hi! Are you there, Karl? Karl!' she yelled as she drew near to the creek, but there was no answering call. In fact no sound at all, except some small animal dashing through the undergrowth.

A cold feeling washed over Jo as she dismounted and let Firefly's reins hang loosely to the ground. A row of she-oaks hid the creekbed from her, but already Jo knew in her heart that nobody was there.

Nevertheless, as she walked out of the trees, her eyes searched for the familiar battered tent and Holden panel van, and the figures of a bent old man and a towsled boy, but they were nowhere to be seen.

'Karl! Grandpa Lofts!' Jo gasped aloud to herself in dismay. 'Oh you couldn't have... you couldn't have done it.'

She scrambled across the gritty creekbed and searched in vain for some sign that they'd be back — a note perhaps, addressed to her, telling her they'd gone temporarily. After all, the ten days were not quite up yet.

But there was nothing. Nothing but a heap of blackened stones, which had served as their fireplace, to tell that they had ever been there.

Jo turned towards a tree and beat the trunk with her fists. 'There's got to be some answer. There's *got* to be!' she said aloud. Then she remembered Grandpa Lofts himself telling her that she ought to stop fighting sometimes and let God help her. She no longer doubted now that somewhere there was a God who loved her. Out of the depths of her heart she cried, 'Oh God, I know that they didn't do it. Help me to prove that they didn't.'

She rose to her feet and began kicking aside tufts of grass carelessly with her boot. Then, suddenly, she noticed on the ground an empty cigarette packet — not stained or torn, but in good condition.

'That's funny,' she said to herself as she stooped and picked it up. 'Grandpa Lofts smokes a pipe and Karl doesn't smoke at all, so somebody else must have been here... somebody who smokes this brand of cigarette... Wow! Of course!'

Suddenly Jo recalled the strange odour she had smelled in the stables last night. It had been cigarette smoke... this very brand, Nickel. The only person she knew who smoked Nickel cigarettes was Mick Fountain.

'Why didn't I think of him before? It could have been Fountain who started the fire to get even with Daddy for sacking him.'

In a few minutes she had returned to where Firefly was waiting and was galloping back to the homestead.

19
Suspects

THE FIRST THING SHE SAW as she rode up was the police car in the drive.

'Aunt Sara! Aunt Sara!' she cried, dashing in, ignoring the policeman.

'Jo,' Aunt Sara placed a restraining hand on her arm. 'I telephoned Sergeant Davies early this morning. He has come to look at the damage. He has already detained the Lofts. He caught them in town just as they were leaving. He has taken them in for questioning, but of course they deny any knowledge of the fire.'

'Sergeant, the Lofts had nothing to do with it! I know that for certain now. I found this down at their camp just now,' Jo burst out, producing the cigarette packet and waving it in the air. 'It belonged to Mick Fountain, I'm positive. He's the only person around here who smoked these.'

'Oh, come on, now, Jo! It could have blown in from the road. After all, the creek is accessible to the road and picnickers do go there from time to time. Besides, Mick Fountain left here the same day as your father went to Brisbane. He's miles away from here by now. I know because I had to go down to Toowoomba on a job a couple of days ago and I saw him in the street — as full as a boot he was,' Sergeant Davies put in gently.

'He was here last night,' Jo said levelly, her cheeks flushing.

'Here? Last night? But you said we were alone except for the Lofts!' Aunt Sara exclaimed aghast.

'Why do you say that?' Sergeant Davies asked evenly.

'Because when I went to the stables, earlier in the evening, I smelled these cigarettes. Only then I didn't take any notice. I was so excited at seeing Firefly again. But Fountain must've been hiding in there then.'

Sergeant Davies and Aunt Sara exchanged wry glances and the sergeant shrugged. 'Well, I'll go along and take a look now,' he said.

'Do you mind if I come, too?' Jo asked, following hard on his heels.

'Suit yourself.' Sergeant Davies called back as he ran down the steps, the dogs clustering around him as he strode towards the ruins of the stables.

'Jo,' Aunt Sara called to her as she was about to shut the screen door, 'do you think you ought to be defending them? I know you owe Karl a lot, but really this is too important an issue to make up stories about it.'

'Aunt Sara, I'm not making up stories. I really did find this cigarette packet down at the Lofts' camp. Obviously Fountain left that way to avoid being seen coming out of our gate. Don't you see? If he wanted people to think he was miles away, he wouldn't leave by the front gate would he? Just think how successful his little plan would have been. He'd have destroyed our prize stallion and filly and our barn — possibly wiped out the whole place — and left all the evidence pointing to the Lofts! And he'd 've got away with it, only we came home. Oh boy! How mad he must have been to see me home! It's a wonder he didn't burn the house down around our ears.

'Yes, Aunt Sara, I really think we had a lucky escape. Or rather, I think God was looking after us.

123

Yes, I really do. I never used to believe in God much once, but lately — well, I've changed my mind. Grandpa Lofts told me the first time I met him that you've got to meet God half-way for him to be able to help you. I think I'm beginning to understand what he meant. I was always so angry at everyone before that God didn't have a chance of getting through.'

When Jo stopped for breath Aunt Sara raised her eyebrows.

'Well, you've made quite a speech there. And it was this Grandpa Lofts, as you call him, who told you this about God?'

Jo nodded. 'Oh he's a real cool guy, Aunt Sara, he really is.'

They were interrupted by footsteps outside and a moment later Sergeant Davies put his head in at the door.

'Thought you'd like to know I found this amongst the rubble on the floor of the stable,' he said as he held out a large green glass bead. 'Looks like the ones Fountain wore on his jacket.'

'There, see, that proves he was here last night,' Jo burst in triumphantly.

'Ah, but did he *lose* it last night? Or a week ago? That's the point, young lady. Or, in fact, did one of the other Dragons lose it when they were here yesterday? However, you might be on the track of something here. Well, I'll be off now ladies. I've work to do,' and, dipping his hat, he walked to his car and drove away.

'I hope for your sake that Fountain did lose it last night,' Aunt Sara said, placing an arm around Jo's shoulders.

Laying her head against her aunt, Jo whispered, 'Thanks Auntie.'

Suddenly Patti managed to spill a glass of milk down the front of her playsuit and she began to cry.

124

'There, there, darling. It's all right,' Aunt Sara turned to comfort the child.

'I'll see to her if you'll put the kettle on, Jo. I could certainly use a cuppa,' said Aunt Sara looking more than a little harrassed as she escorted Patti to the bedroom.

Two hours later Sergeant Davies rang. Aunt Sara answered the phone and, when she had finished speaking, she came into the kitchen where Jo was making a batch of pikelets.

'They've found Fountain,' she said, pausing mysteriously.

'Where? Where? Come on, don't keep me in suspense. Did he admit to anything?' Jo burst out.

'Yes, he's made a statement. He was found in a gully all beaten and bruised with a couple of broken ribs. He's in the hospital right now,' said Aunt Sara bluntly, adding, 'It looks as if his friends finally caught up with him.'

'Oh, no!' gasped Jo, turning pale. 'Was he responsible for the fire?'

'Yes, he's admitted it. The police had narrowed it down to him anyway because they'd caught up with the other two Dragons and Fountain is the only one with an eye missing from his jacket.'

'From what Sergeant Davies could make out, the two who came here yesterday were after Fountain because he had skipped out on them, owing them quite a bit of money. They asked around town and, when they found out that Fountain hadn't been seen for nearly a week, decided that Mrs Banks must have been telling the truth. But, because they didn't like her threatening to set the police on to them, they decided to come back here and 'have a rumble' as they put it.

'Fortunately for us, however, one of them had a mishap with his bike which forced them to stay in town till it was fixed by the mechanic at the all-night

125

road house. They met up with the driver of a semi-trailer who told them he had given a chap wearing a Dragon jacket a ride to within about thirty kilometres of town, where he'd asked to be let off as he had a 'job' to go to.

'By the time the other two Dragons got out here they must have seen the glow of the fire from the road and thought better of coming any closer, but decided to sit and wait for Fountain to appear. One of them apparently kept the gate covered and the other went down the side road towards the picnic ground by the creek.

'Sure enough, Fountain finally appeared via the creek where, to his surprise, he found his ex-mate, who must have picked him up on the pretext of giving him a lift out of the district. Instead, though, he took him to Talbot's gully, where he was met a few minutes later by the other fellow. They were able to settle their score, leaving Fountain badly injured.'

'Wow!', breathed Jo when her Aunt Sara had stopped. 'What a story! And Karl and Grandpa Lofts — what about them?'

'Well, they're in the clear now,' Aunt Sara stopped. 'I guess you were right after all,' she added softly, after a minute.

'Oh Auntie, isn't that great! I knew they hadn't started the fire,' Jo said excitedly.

'Yes, Jo, it certainly is,' agreed her aunt. Then she went on, 'According to Sergeant Davies, Mr Lofts said he heard a motorcycle roaring in the distance about eleven o'clock but he didn't take much notice. After all, occasionally people take that turn by mistake and end up down by the creek. Or it could have been someone out shooting. He said the fellow didn't stay long though and after ten minutes he seemed to turn around and go back to the road.

'So that's about it,' she finished with a shrug, adding with a twinkle in her eye, 'Except that Sergeant Davies also told me that the Lofts are about to leave town for the opal fields.'

'Oh Auntie, they mustn't. Please take me into town,' Jo begged.

'Okay, what are we waiting for? Let's get the babies and be off,' Aunt Sara winked, and ten minutes later they were burning down the track in a manner that would have appalled Jo's father had he seen them.

After a fruitless search around town for the Lofts' old Holden panel van, Aunt Sara turned her car towards the west.

Sure enough, twelve kilometres down the road they caught up with the blue van, belching smoke from its exhaust as it made hard work of the journey. They drew ahead of it and stopped.

'Karl! Grandpa Lofts!' Jo called, jumping from the car. 'Don't go, please don't go!'

'What's this?' Grandpa Lofts peered at Jo through his open window. 'How'd you git here, young lady?'

'My aunt brought me. This is my Aunt Sara,' she drew back and indicated Aunt Sara standing behind her.

Politely Grandpa Lofts dipped his hat to Aunt Sara, then turned back to Jo. 'So the prodigal has returned, eh?' The old man smiled and brushed a fly away from his nose. 'They told us back at the police station that you were back and about the fire.' Grandpa Lofts stopped and looked serious.

'Oh, Grandpa Lofts, we didn't suspect you. I didn't, not for a minute,' Jo burst out.

'I'm afraid that I did, Mr Lofts. And. . . I, I'm sorry,' Aunt Sara said firmly.

Sadly the old man shook his head. 'Don't make no difference now. We're on the move — heading for the boulder opal out Quilpie way. Just heard there's fellas becoming millionaires overnight by a single strike of the pick.'

'Pa!' Karl put in, in mock disgust. 'That's a story, and you know it!'

'Not a story, lad. A dream perhaps, but not a story,' the old man sighed.

'Pa, why can't we stay?' Karl put in earnestly.

'Course we can't lad. Our time's up and we gotta push on,' the old man turned to him almost roughly.

'Oh, don't worry about your time being up. My Dad said you can stay a while longer. You see, I told him I'd come home and get the planting started for him, but I can't do it alone. I thought you and Karl might be willing to help. There's a cottage to live in, and my dad will sort out about your pay.' Jo stopped, feeling embarrassed.

'You want some help did you say? Planting wheat? Why, I grew up on a wheat farm. There ain't nothing I can do better than plant wheat,' Grandpa Lofts grinned widely from ear to ear.

'Well then, you'll stay till it's finished at least? It's all settled then? You'll work for us?' Jo put out her hand and Grandpa Lofts took it and shook it.

'It's a deal.' He winked at her then added, 'Only I'd like to be independent. We'll camp on the creek again if it's all the same to you.'

'Sure,' Jo shrugged and Karl made a thumbs-up sign at her, which meant that things couldn't have turned out better.

20
Jo's choice

FOR THE NEXT TWO WEEKS Aunt Sara and the little girls saw very little of Jo during the day. Breakfast was a whirlwind rush in the mornings and, after school, Jo scarcely had time to say 'hello' and grab a snack before, changing into her working clothes, she was off to help Grandpa Lofts and Karl with the planting.

Then one day Mrs McIntosh rang to say her husband would not be coming back to work on Tinoonan, as the doctor had advised against it. She was very apologetic, but definite.

'Wouldn't mind working on the land again meself,' Grandpa Lofts said wistfully that day as they took a breather.

'Well, why don't you come and work for my Dad permanently? He'll be really short-handed with Mr McIntosh not coming back and Fountain gone. And anyway I'm sure you and Karl between you could handle the work Fountain did. That is, after Karl has finished school in the afternoon,' she added, her eyes twinkling.

'Has he been talking to you about being a mining engineer one day, like his Dad?' Grandpa Lofts pulled on his pipe as he looked at Jo.

'Well, he did mention it once,' Jo admitted, 'but he said he wouldn't be able to leave you alone all day to do the heavy digging.' She paused.

'Wouldn't he just?' Grandpa Lofts exploded.

'Well, let's hear none of that talk, now young fella-me-lad. You stay fossicking 'cause you wants to fossick, understand? Not just to please an old man.'

'Gee, Pa, you mean you don't mind if I stay on at school?' Karl butted in, his eyes aglow. 'But I can't leave you to do the heavy work.'

'It's your life, son. You must choose,' Grandpa Lofts said solemnly. 'I ain't never been much of a one for higher education. Got by most of me life without it. But I know it's different today.'

He sighed. 'But as for staying on here — get such ideas out of your head. As soon as we've finished this contract with Jo here, we've got to move on. I've promised her Dad. And I'm a man of me word.'

Jo and Karl exchanged crestfallen glances. They had both secretly been hoping that somehow the adults would change their attitude toward each other.

It was Jo's birthday and, the planting being finished, Jo and Aunt Sara had decided to take Patti and Claire for a picnic by the dam. At Aunt Sara's invitation they had been joined for lunch by Grandpa Lofts and Karl. The children had a wonderful time cray-fishing and swimming in the muddy dam water. And then, on Aunt Sara's further insistence, the Lofts were invited to the homestead for a farewell tea. Farewell, because Grandpa Lofts had decided that, now that the job was completed, they really must be moving on.

When they arrived back at the homestead, however, a strange Ford station wagon was drawn up beside the house gate.

'Whoever can that belong to?' gasped Jo, pointing to the strange car. 'And where's the driver?'

Just then Fiona came rushing out of the house. 'Surprise! Surprise!' she called, flinging her arms around Jo's neck, then turning to hug Patti and take baby Claire from Aunt Sara.

Jo felt tears stinging her eyes — to think that Fiona had hugged her first. . . she couldn't get over it.

And then she saw the tall gaunt figure of her father filling the back doorway. He was leaning heavily on a stick, but his face was wreathed in smiles as he held out a hand to Jo.

'Pretty good place you run here, boss,' he said with a twinkle in his eye. 'And I hear you had a fire a couple of weeks ago and got the horses out single-handed, to say nothing of saving the barn!'

'Oh Dad, what a wonderful surprise!' Jo exclaimed, laughing and crying at the same time as he hugged her.

'Well, aren't you going to ask us to come in?' Aunt Sara said at last when the talking died down.

Mr Lacey took a step backward and gestured for the others to enter.

'We'll be on our way, then, Miss Lacey,' Grandpa Lofts began awkwardly, but Jo's father overheard him.

'Indeed you won't,' he gestured for Grandpa Lofts and Karl to follow the others in. 'Come on in. I've been wanting to see you,' he went on, looking Grandpa Lofts straight in the eye.

'Mr Lofts, I believe I owe you an apology,' he began humbly.

'Not at all, not at all,' Grandpa Lofts began, embarrassed.

Mr Lacey put out his hand to quiet him. 'No, please, let me go on. I know if it were not for your grandson here, I may have lost not only one, but two of my daughters. And I want to thank him for being here when he was needed. I'm sorry I misjudged you and even thought you could be responsible for causing harm to my property. I want you to know that I am rescinding the order I gave you three weeks ago to leave here. Now I am asking you, no, begging you to stay. In fact, I would be most happy if you would be willing to work for me permanently on Tinoonan.'

'Oh, you can do some prospecting from time to time if you wish, but I'd like you to work for me in place of Fountain, especially now Fred McIntosh has also gone. Jo wrote that you came off the land many years ago, Mr Lofts, and as I'm going to be out of action for many weeks yet, I sure would appreciate experienced help. I'd also appreciate it if you'd consider moving into the men's quarters, which are lying idle. They're quite comfortable; no palace, mind you, but comfortable...'

'Wow! A house of our own!' Karl let out a yell.

Grandpa Lofts, who preferred to live in a tent any day, took one look at Karl's ecstatic face and said, 'I'm most honoured to accept your kind offer, sir.'

'And Karl, young man, as I won't be up to riding for months, I would sure appreciate it if you would take over looking after King for me. That's when Jo's given you a few more lessons, of course,' he added with a wink in Jo's direction.

'Aw great! Thanks Mr Lacey,' Karl's face glowed with pleasure which was only equalled by the glow on Jo's.

'Thanks, Dad, for not being angry about that,' Jo breathed.

'Thank you, Jo, for the capable manner in which you've looked after things while I've been away. In fact you've done such a good job that from now on I'm going to keep you on as my part-time assistant. And one of our first jobs together, when I am well again, will be to thin out the 'roos.' Jo's father raised one eyebrow quizzically as he spoke.

'Far out!' Jo laughed excitedly, 'and can Karl come too?'

Mr Lacey nodded. 'I guess so. After all it's part of the work of running this place.'

'Oh Karl, isn't it terrific the way everything has turned out?' Jo turned to Karl who clicked his tongue and made another thumbs-up sign, which this time meant that as far as he was concerned everything was simply perfect.

Suddenly Jo turned to Grandpa Lofts. 'I take back what I said to you the day I first met you about God not caring what happened to me. I sure know different now,' she whispered.

As she looked up into the old man's eyes, she was surprised to see tears glistening there.

'Well, now that all the business is settled, let's get on with that birthday party, eh? I think Fiona has a cake hidden somewhere. I know, because I was nursing it all the way from Brisbane,' said Mr Lacey, clapping his hands together in a let's-get-on-with-it way.

Just then the telephone rang and Aunt Sara went to answer it. A moment later she was back. 'It's for you, Jo,' she said, looking a little strange.

'It's probably one of my friends from school,' Jo rose to her feet and hastily left the room.

'Hi!' she said, picking up the phone.

'Joanna, I just had to wish you a happy birthday.'

Jo gave a little gasp. 'Mother!' she exclaimed.

'Well, don't sound so surprised. I am your mum after all. And now that I've met you, darling, I don't want to lose contact altogether.'

Jo was speechless. From the dining room came the sound of a happy conversation. Then above the murmur of voices Patti's shrill treble rang out, demanding to know when the party was going to begin.

'Mother...'

'Call me Mum, sweetie,' her mother cut in, 'Mother sounds much too staid.'

'Gee, Mum, I don't know what to say. It's such a... a lovely surprise to hear your voice. Are you ringing from Sydney?' Jo breathed, her voice suddenly hoarse.

'Yes, sweetie, I've been thinking such a lot about you since the night you turned up at the TV station, and to make up for all the birthdays I've missed I want you to come with me on a cruise to Fiji during your school holidays next month. Think of it — just you and me together. You'd like that, wouldn't you? I've checked out the dates and have made arrangements with my agent to keep those two weeks free.' She paused for breath.

'Like it! Fiji!' breathed Jo, her mind conjuring up pictures of palm trees swaying and native girls dancing. Wouldn't she just be the envy of all the kids at school! And with her mother all to herself! It was beyond her wildest dreams.

'Well, what do you say, honey?' her mother's voice went on, as a strange voice cut in and announced, 'Three minutes — are you extending?'

'Yes, yes please,' Jo heard her mother say impatiently. Then, 'Joanna, are you still there?' she asked.

'Yes, yes I'm here. Well, Mother... that is, Mum, it sounds groovy. But what about... Richard?' Jo stopped.

'Oh don't worry about him. I've told him about you and he's quite ready to accept the fact that he'll have a daughter. As a matter of fact he's in favour of the cruise, so long as I go incognito. He says it's a chance for us to get to know each other. And in case you're worried about your father, I've already asked his permission and it's okay.'

From her own experience Jo wondered if Richard would indeed find accepting her all that easy, but in her excitement she brushed the complication aside.

'It'd be fantastic,' she began.

Suddenly, from the next room her father's laugh rang out, resonant and jolly. It was such a reassuring sound, and the realisation that she might never have heard it again suddenly hit Jo with new force. All at once she knew that she couldn't bear to be parted from her Dad, not so soon anyway. Not even to be with her mother. Besides, while he was not well he needed her to help with the work.

'Look, Mum, I'm afraid I couldn't come... not these next holidays. Maybe at the end of the year,' her voice trailed away.

'But Joanna, why ever not? I've made tentative arrangements and I can't get away later in the year, not alone anyway,' Jo's mother burst in petulantly. Then she began to coax, 'Look, you don't have to decide straightaway. Think it over and let me know later. Your father has my address. I want you to come, Jo. I want you to very much.'

Jo tried to explain that her father was just home — that she owed it to him to help on Tinoonan right now — that some other time she'd love to come. But it was no use. Her mother couldn't, or wouldn't, understand.

As Jo rang off with promises to keep in touch, she was aware of the bewilderment in her mother's voice, and it made her feel inexpressibly sad. But in her heart she knew she had made the right decision.

Slowly Jo replaced the receiver and walked back to the dining room. Her father looked at her inquiringly as she came through the door.

'It was my Mum. She wanted to take me on a cruise to Fiji.'

'Yes, I know,' her father nodded.

'I told her I wouldn't be able to... not these next holidays. Because they're going to be very special.' She paused, then looking her father directly in the eye she went on, 'God's given us a second chance, Dad, and at the moment all I want is to be with you

135

and Fiona and the kids — and to get on with living like a proper family.' Her voice shook with emotion as she reached out and squeezed her father's hand hard.

'Oh Jo!' her father whispered as he returned the squeeze. For a moment everyone was silent.

Then 'Come on, come on! On with the party,' Mr Lacey called as Fiona came from the kitchen carrying a beautiful pink frosted birthday cake which she placed in the centre of the table. On the top of the cake was an inscription. Jo craned her head to read it. It said 'Happy Birthday, Jo, Love — Fiona and Dad'.

As Jo glanced around the table at all of those whom she loved most in the world, her heart sang with happiness. Surely, surely she had found her land where the rainbow ends. Looking Fiona straight in the eye, she said simply, 'Thank you, Fiona, for everything.'

In the corner, Grandpa Lofts quietly bowed his head in a little prayer of thanks.

'Come on, let's light the candles,' Patti cried, clapping her hands.

'Shush, Patti,' her mother answered, 'you have to eat your tea first. Then we'll all drink a toast to Jo.'